BLACK AND BLUEBERRY DIE

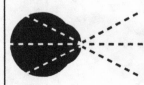

This Large Print Book carries the
Seal of Approval of N.A.V.H.

A FRESH BAKED MYSTERY

BLACK AND BLUEBERRY DIE

LIVIA J. WASHBURN

WHEELER PUBLISHING
A part of Gale, a Cengage Company

GALE
A Cengage Company

Farmington Hills, Mich • San Francisco • New York • Waterville, Maine
Meriden, Conn • Mason, Ohio • Chicago

GALE
A Cengage Company

LIBRARY OF CONGRESS CIP DATA ON FILE.
CATALOGUING IN PUBLICATION FOR THIS BOOK
IS AVAILABLE FROM THE LIBRARY OF CONGRESS

ISBN-13: 978-1-4328-4579-7 (softcover)
ISBN-10: 1-4328-4579-9 (softcover)

Published in 2018 by arrangement with Livia J. Washburn

Printed in Mexico
1 2 3 4 5 6 7 22 21 20 19 18

Dedicated to my husband, James, and my daughters, Joanna and Shayna, for helping keep me sane. (Hush you three, snickering is rude!) And to the memory of my parents, Paul and Naomi Washburn, who ran Paul's Beauty Shop for many years before Mom went back to school to get a teaching degree. Those memories of growing up in a beauty shop are fond ones.

CHAPTER 1

Phyllis Newsom fanned herself with the church bulletin from that morning's service and said, "Can you believe that people used to live without air conditioning?"

Sam Fletcher stretched his legs out in front of him and crossed them at the ankles. He was wearing a Texas Rangers t-shirt and blue jean shorts and his feet were bare. Next to Sam's chair on the porch lay Buck, the Dalmatian he had rescued from the local animal shelter. Buck's chin rested on his front paws, a picture of contentment since he was with his human.

"I thought you were fond of the good ol' days," Sam said to Phyllis with a smile on his craggy face. "You're always talkin' about 'em."

"I suppose I am . . . but there's no need to be fanatical about these things."

Phyllis wore sandals, capri pants, and a short-sleeved, lightweight blouse. Her mother never would have dressed like that on the Sabbath and probably would have disapproved of the outfit on her daughter. But as far as Phyllis was concerned, this was perfectly fine attire for a warm September Sunday afternoon at home. She was a grown woman, too, she reminded herself. Quite a few decades *beyond* being a grown woman, in fact.

"When's the fella comin' to fix the A/C?" Sam asked.

"He said he'd be here sometime tomorrow."

"Mornin' or afternoon?"

"Sometime tomorrow," Phyllis repeated. "That's as much as he could narrow it down. And I got the feeling he thought I should be grateful he'd be here that soon."

"How busy can he be this late in the season?"

"It's still warm enough to need the air conditioner, isn't it? It won't really cool off much until next month, and I suspect we'll still be running the air conditioner even then."

"Heater in the mornin', air conditioner in the afternoon, that's Texas for you," Sam said. "Speakin' of that, when I was growin' up, we had a gas furnace for the winter and window units for the summer. Swamp coolers, at that. I think I was nearly grown before my folks ever bought an air conditioner with freon in it."

Phyllis leaned her head toward the house and said, "That's the way it was here when Kenny and I moved in, until we got it all replaced with the central unit."

"Well, I'll be glad when it's fixed. You get used to things."

"That's true," Phyllis said.

For example, she was used to Sam's company. It was hard to believe that only a few years earlier, she didn't even know him, let alone consider him her best friend. She hadn't been sure about renting him a room here in this big old house on a tree-shaded side street in Weatherford, Texas. Now she knew it was one of the best decisions she'd ever made.

The front door opened and Carolyn Wilbarger came out onto the porch carrying a tray with a pitcher and several glasses on it. Condensation heavily beaded the sides of the pitcher, which was full of ice and a pale yellow liquid.

"Fresh lemonade," Carolyn announced.

Sam grinned and said, "That sounds mighty good. You're next thing to an angel right now, Carolyn."

"I thought you two might need some cooling off."

Sam's grin widened as he asked in a mischievous tone, "Why, whatever do you mean by that, Miz Wilbarger?"

Carolyn ignored the question. She placed the tray on a small plastic table between the rocking chairs where Phyllis and Sam sat, filled one of the glasses with cold lemonade, and thrust it into Sam's hand.

"Here. Just drink that."

Sam took a swallow, licked his lips, and nodded appreciatively. "Tart but sorta sweet, too. Hits the spot, that's for sure."

Carolyn poured lemonade into the other two glasses, handed one to Phyllis, and then sat down with her glass in one of the other rocking chairs.

"At least there's a nice breeze out here," she said. "It's like an oven in that kitchen." She laughed. "Well, you know what I mean."

"I certainly do," Phyllis said. "By the way, I got an email from Eve this morning."

Their friend Eve Turner, who also rented a room here, had sold a novel the previous year, and now there was talk about turning it into a movie, which meant Eve had had to go to California to discuss the deal.

"Is she all right?" Carolyn rolled her eyes and shook her head. "I can't imagine her on the loose out there in Hollywood. Well, actually, I *can* imagine. That's the trouble."

"She's fine," Phyllis said. "She should be back later this week if everything goes as planned."

"They still gettin' ready to make that movie outta her book?" Sam asked.

"Who knows? She says nothing is ever settled in Hollywood until all the contracts are signed, and even then you can't be sure. But I think she's having a fine time just talking to the studio executives about it and having them make a fuss over her."

"Yes, she'd enjoy that," Carolyn said. "Mark my words, she'll wind up married to some big-shot Hollywood producer."

Sam scratched his jaw and said, "Who do you think they'll get to play me?"

"Tom Baxter in the book isn't you," Phyllis said. "None of those characters are us. They're just very loosely inspired by us."

"Loosely inspired, my hind foot," Carolyn said. "A bunch of retired schoolteachers sharing a house and solving murders in a small Texas town. How much closer to reality could it be?"

"I was thinkin' maybe Sam Elliott," Sam went on. "On account of us havin' the same first name and all. Not to mention the rugged good looks."

Phyllis sat up straighter and placed her

half-full glass of lemonade on the table. She had spotted a police car coming down the street. A sheriff's department car, actually, and now it eased to a stop at the curb in front of the yard.

"Mike's here," Carolyn announced unnecessarily. She stood up. "I'll go get another glass."

"He may not have time for lemonade," Phyllis said.

"Everybody has time for lemonade on a hot afternoon, even a deputy sheriff."

With that declaration, Carolyn disappeared into the house.

Phyllis's son Mike got out of the car and came up the walk. He wore his deputy's uniform. Phyllis didn't know if he was on his way to work or was already on duty. Either way he probably wouldn't be able to stay long, but she was glad to see him anyway.

"Hi, Mom, hi, Sam," he said as he stopped with one foot on the first of the three steps leading up to the porch. "Why are you sitting out here?"

"Can't people enjoy a pleasant Sunday afternoon?" Phyllis said.

"A/C conked out," Sam said.

"Have you got somebody coming to fix it?"

"He'll be here tomorrow," Phyllis said.

Mike nodded. "Okay. But if it gets too hot, you know you can come stay with us. It's usually . . . Never mind."

Sam nodded toward Mike and said to Phyllis, "He was about to say it's usually old people who die from gettin' overheated, I'll bet."

Phyllis ignored that and said, "You looked a little worried about something before you even knew our air conditioner was out, Mike. Is something wrong?"

Her son's face was solemn now, but even though something appeared to be bothering him, he seemed reluctant to share it. After a moment, he said, "This was probably a bad idea."

"Coming to see your mother is never a bad idea."

Mike took a deep breath and said, "It is when you're coming to ask her to get mixed up in a murder case."

"You remember Danny Jackson," Mike said a short time later. He was sitting in one of the rockers with his own glass of lemonade. Carolyn had been right about that.

"Of course," Phyllis said. "I was sorry to hear about what happened. It was really hard to believe."

13

"I went over to Fort Worth this morning to talk to him. They're still holding him in the jail there. He should have been transferred to the penitentiary in Huntsville by now, but there's some sort of hold-up in the paperwork."

"Got to have all the right papers and tell the computers exactly what they want to hear," Sam said. "Otherwise you can't get anything done this day and age."

"Well, in this case bureaucracy may have actually accomplished something good, even if it was by accident, because Danny had a chance to call me and tell me he wanted to talk to me." Mike frowned. "I hadn't seen him in four or five years. We're friends on Facebook, but we hadn't actually talked . . . Anyway, I didn't think it would be a very good idea, a sheriff's deputy visiting a convicted murderer in jail, but he sounded really desperate. And then he played the eighty yard run card."

"The eighty yard run card?" Sam repeated.

Mike nodded. "Final game of the season my senior year. We were playing Stephenville, and whoever won would be district champs. The score was tied late in the game, and we had the ball on our own nineteen yard line. It was third and eleven, and we

14

couldn't try to throw for a first down because our quarterback had a rubber band for an arm. So he hands the ball to me on a sweep, and Danny, who's playing right tackle, makes the best block you'll ever see in your life. Takes out their defensive end and *two* linebackers. I got outside, juked the defensive back who came up, and realized that not only was I going to get the first down, if I could get past the safety I had a clear shot down the sideline." Mike shrugged. "So I ran over him and was off to the races."

"I remember that game," Phyllis said. "It was one of the most exciting things I ever saw."

"But you were on your nineteen, you said . . ." Sam commented.

"Yeah, the DB I put a move on finally caught up to me and brought me down at the Stephenville one. Our quarterback snuck in on the next play, and that was the game. But I never would have gone for eighty and basically won the game if it hadn't been for Danny's block."

"I understood a little of that," Carolyn said. "You're saying you owed this man a debt."

"A big one. Because that was the night I finally got up the courage to ask Sarah to

15

go out with me, and . . . well . . ."

"And now you're married and have a beautiful son and of course you feel grateful to Danny for whatever small part he might have played in you and Sarah getting together," Phyllis said. "But still, he killed his wife."

"That's just it, Mom," Mike said. "I'm not convinced he did."

CHAPTER 2

Phyllis was telling the truth when she said she remembered Danny Jackson. It would have been hard for her to forget the boy who had been her son's best friend all the way through junior high and high school. Danny and Mike had set at Phyllis's own kitchen table many times eating peanut butter and jelly sandwiches or hot dogs or bowls of ice cream. She had driven them to football practice and Little League games and Boy Scout meetings. They had set in the living room watching sports on TV with Kenny, Mike's dad and Phyllis's late husband. Danny's dad wasn't in the picture — Phyllis didn't know the details and hadn't had any reason to pry into the boy's home life — so Kenny had, at times, been like a surrogate father to him. To tell the truth, Phyllis remembered all of it vividly, more so than many of the things that had happened recently.

Of course, time had passed and best friends or not, the lives of the two young men had taken different courses. Mike had gone to college, majored in criminal justice, and become a sheriff's deputy. Danny had gone to college, too, but only for a year before enlisting in the Army. He'd been deployed somewhere overseas but hadn't seen any combat as far as Phyllis knew. After two "hitches" — Phyllis supposed they still called them that — he had returned to civilian life, gotten married to a girl he had dated while he was in college, and settled down in Fort Worth, evidently happy and ready to get on with his life.

Phyllis heard about those things in passing from Mike, but she remembered them well enough she'd been shocked when she heard, some months earlier, that Danny had been arrested for the murder of his wife.

"You know how when something bad happens, people always say they never knew it was coming?" Mike said.

"They used to say that," Sam responded. "Now most folks say, 'Oh, yeah, I always knew he was crazy and was gonna snap one of these days.' "

Mike shrugged and nodded. "Unfortunately, that's true. It *does* seem like we have more obviously crazy and violent people these days. But in Danny and Roxanne's case it was more of a surprise. They seemed happy. I saw the pictures both of them posted on Facebook. They were always doing things together and looked like they were in love."

With her usual cynicism, Carolyn said, "Married couples get in the habit of *looking* like they're in love. It makes things simpler and easier that way, whether it's true or not."

"I guess. I'm sure Danny and Roxanne had their problems. But if anybody had told me he was going to kill her, especially like . . . that . . . I would have said they were nuts."

"She was beaten to death, wasn't she?" Phyllis asked quietly.

Mike nodded. "Blunt force trauma. In fact, it was bad enough that, well, they had a little trouble identifying her."

Carolyn leaned forward in her rocking chair and asked, "Were the authorities absolutely certain it was her who was killed? I mean, could it have been some other woman about the same age and shape and size . . . ?"

"Her fingerprints were on file because she had a license to carry a gun. It was her, all right. No doubt about it. That other sort of thing only happens in books and movies."

Phyllis frowned slightly and said, "Why would she carry a gun? Was she afraid of something . . . or someone?"

"Like Danny?" Mike shook his head. "No. Sometimes Roxanne closed up at the beauty parlor where she worked and took the day's deposit to the bank. She just kept a little pistol in the car because of that and being out after dark. I doubt if she ever fired it except now and then on the range."

"You said Danny wanted to talk to you," Sam put in. "What did he tell you? Did he claim he was innocent?"

"He did. He said he loved Roxanne and never would have hurt her. But . . . he's the one who found her body at the beauty shop and called 911. He was pretty disoriented when the cops got there —"

"Well, I would expect so," Carolyn said, "if he found his wife murdered, after all."

"But in any homicide where the victim is married, the spouse is always the first suspect," Mike said. His face was grim. "Danny had a lot of . . . DNA evidence on him —"

"You mean Roxanne's blood," Phyllis said.

Mike sighed and nodded. "Yeah. He was covered with it. And he didn't have any sort of alibi. Plus there were witnesses who said

20

that Danny and Roxanne *had* been having trouble in their marriage after all, no matter what it looked like to their old friends. That was enough for Danny to be arrested and indicted. Why would the police look that hard at anybody else? I don't think our detectives would have."

"There was no one to testify on his behalf at the trial?"

"A few character witnesses," Mike said with a shrug, "but nothing to contradict the physical evidence or discredit the few witnesses the state called. The trial really didn't amount to much. The jury deliberated less than an hour. Danny was sentenced to thirty years for second-degree murder."

Sam asked, "What did he say to make you think he's not guilty? You've dealt with enough criminals to know that plenty of 'em deny what they did, up one way and down the other, even when they've been caught red-handed."

"He told me he and Roxanne were about to go away together on a second honeymoon. More like a first one, actually, since they didn't have much of a honeymoon when they first got married because Danny had just gotten out of the army and they didn't have any money. Anyway, they were going to Las Vegas because they could afford it now, and Danny just sounded so . . . so happy about it. Even in jail, when he talked about what could have been, he sounded like it would have been wonderful. And then he started to cry." Mike shook his head. "I just can't believe he'd hurt her."

Phyllis said, "People sometimes do things in the heat of an argument that they would never do otherwise."

"I know. Believe me, I've worked in law enforcement long enough to know there's no limit to the terrible things people will do, even when you think they never would. If somebody else was telling me this story about their friend and said that he couldn't possibly be a murderer, I'd be skeptical. But . . . it's me, and it's Danny, and I believe him."

For a long moment, none of them said anything. Then Phyllis asked, "Did Danny want you to come and talk to me about the case, Mike?"

He nodded. "Yeah. He knew I couldn't do anything to help him, that it would be a conflict of interest and could get me in trouble. But of course he'd heard about you and some of the things you've done . . . I guess most people around here have heard about that. You're kind of a celebrity, Mom, whether you like it or not."

Phyllis *didn't* like it. She had never set out to be a detective. She had lived nearly all of her life without ever solving any sort of mystery, other than figuring out who might have been cheating on tests in her eighth grade history class.

Then, over the past few years, what had been a pleasant retirement surrounded by friends and family had been disrupted by a series of crimes in which Phyllis had had no choice but to get involved. To help those she cared about, she had investigated those murders and eventually turned up the guilty party. She had been suspected of various things and even wound up in jail herself for a short time, but everything had always turned out all right in the end. At least, as all right as it could have, considering some of the tragic things that had occurred.

Mike went on, "Danny said he always thought it was cool that his best friend's mom solved all those murders, but he never dreamed he would need you to help him someday."

"He wants me to investigate his wife's death."

"It's not an open case anymore," Mike pointed out. "You wouldn't get in any trouble with the law for poking around some." He shook his head. "I hate to ask it, especially after I've spent all these years, well, fussing at you for getting mixed up in these things . . ."

Carolyn said, "You were just trying to look out for your mother. There's nothing wrong with that."

Sam said, "At least the crime took place in Fort Worth. The Weatherford cops and the Parker County sheriff don't have anything to do with it."

"I don't really know that much about the case," Phyllis said. "Just what you told me and what I read about it in the newspaper. I never even met Danny's wife. I'm not sure where I'd start."

"Just think it over," Mike said. "If you don't want to get involved, that's perfectly all right. I understand completely." He drank the rest of the lemonade in his glass and stood up. "I have to get moving. My shift starts pretty soon."

"I will think about it," Phyllis promised.

"Thanks, Mom." Mike bent and kissed her forehead.

"Give my love to Sarah and Bobby."

"Sure." Mike lifted a hand in farewell. "So long, Sam. Thanks for the lemonade, Miz Wilbarger."

He got in the sheriff's cruiser and drove away. As they watched the car roll on down the street, Carolyn said to Phyllis, "If you don't help his friend, it's not going to be perfectly all right and he won't understand completely, no matter what he says."

"I don't know," Sam said. "Mike's not the sort to hold a grudge." He shrugged. "Still, when fellas play ball together, there's a bond between 'em. It's not like bein' in combat with somebody, of course, but to a much lesser degree, there's a feelin' like you've gone to war together."

"You're both saying I should investigate Roxanne Jackson's murder," Phyllis said. "But what if I do, and I come to the conclusion that Danny really *is* guilty? That's going to be awfully hard for Mike to accept."

"At least he'll know for sure," Sam said. "That's got to be a good thing in the long run. It'd be hard to spend the rest of your life havin' doubts about something like that. It might gnaw at him to think he hadn't done everything he could to help an old friend."

Phyllis nodded and said, "That's true." She sighed. "It doesn't appear that I have much choice. You know, enough time has gone by since that trouble last Christmas that I thought I'd never have to deal with any murders again."

"And now you're right back at it." Sam

grinned. "You know the old sayin' about how the more things change —"

"The more Phyllis Newsom is up to her neck in murder," Carolyn said.

CHAPTER 3

When Phyllis was growing up, her parents always had a set of encyclopedias in the house, which she knew made her luckier than some children. Whenever she needed to look something up for her school work, she hadn't had to go to the library or wait until she was back in the classroom, which had its own encyclopedias. She could do her research right at home.

She'd also been the sort of kid who would sit and read an encyclopedia for fun, which led more than once to her being called a weirdo and a bookworm, but she didn't really care about that. Learning mattered more.

She wondered if people these days still bought encyclopedias. She had a set, but they were close to twenty years old and she hadn't given any thought to replacing them.

Probably she could find a newer set cheap somewhere on the Internet, she mused as she sat down at the computer in the living room that evening.

But encyclopedias wouldn't tell her anything about Roxanne Jackson's murder. For that she had to rely on what Sam called "Google-fu".

Since Roxanne had been a beautician and her husband ran a paint and body shop, there hadn't been a lot of media coverage about her murder. As a firm believer in the idea that all human lives were important, Phyllis didn't think that was fair, but she was also pragmatic enough to know it was true. The case had received a little interest because Roxanne had been killed in an upscale salon on the west side of Fort Worth patronized by a number of old-money clients who lived in the area, but the media would have paid a lot more attention if it had been one of those wealthy matrons who'd wound up dead, not the young woman who did their hair.

Danny and Roxanne had lived in the country, west of the loop that ran around Fort Worth. They had bought an old farmhouse set back about a quarter of a mile from the county road and remodeled it themselves. Danny was handy about things like that, and Roxanne had pitched in willingly to help.

On the night of Roxanne's murder, Danny had worked late at his shop to finish up a job, but he'd been there alone, his partner having left earlier. There were no witnesses to prove when he'd left the shop. Knowing that Roxanne was also working late, he had stopped and gotten take-out food for them, then decided to drive by the salon and see if she was still there. He hadn't really thought she would be, but seeing her car still in the parking lot, he had stopped and gone in to see if she was all right.

Unfortunately, Roxanne had been far from all right.

The police had found the paper sack of cold burgers and fries sitting on the floor just inside the salon's unlocked door. Later, during questioning, Danny had said that he dropped them there in shock when he walked in and found his wife's bloody, battered corpse lying in front of the hair dryers.

He had run and knelt beside her and grabbed her to see if she was alive. That was how he had come to get her blood all over his hands and shirt. All he could think was that someone had broken into the place to rob it and found Roxanne there, causing the intruder to panic and kill her. It was a story that could have been true . . .

"Figured that's what I'd find you doin'," Sam said from behind Phyllis. He moved gracefully and quietly, as always, like the athlete he had once been, but she didn't jump in surprise. Sam's voice never made her do that.

"Well, I told Mike I would think about it," she said, "and I can't really do that unless I have the facts of the case."

"I got the dishwasher loaded," Sam said as he stepped up beside her chair. That was one of the jobs he usually tried to take care of. He rested his left hand lightly on her right shoulder and went on, "Findin' out much?"

Phyllis sighed and shook her head.

"Not really." Quickly, she sketched in what she had learned so far, then continued, "Unfortunately, that's about all there is to it. The newspaper story says evidence at the scene led police to believe that Danny was involved in his wife's death, but it doesn't go into detail about what that evidence was. There's also a mention that the marriage was 'troubled', whatever that means, but again the story doesn't elaborate."

"Carolyn would probably say all marriages are troubled."

Phyllis looked around to make sure her old friend wasn't in earshot, then said

30

quietly, "Carolyn takes a jaundiced view of a lot of things. She's probably right, though, just not to the degree she believes she is. No marriage runs smoothly all the time."

Sam shrugged and said, "I reckon that's true, unless the two people just flat don't give a damn about each other anymore. It's hard to work up the energy to fight if you don't really care."

"I suppose." Phyllis couldn't imagine such a thing. "Anyway, I'm not sure there's anything here to go on. I can't even make a guess about whether the police misinterpreted the evidence when I don't know what the evidence was."

"It would be in the trial transcript, wouldn't it?"

"It would have to be. The prosecution made enough of a case for the jury to convict Danny almost right away."

"Trials are public," Sam pointed out.

"Yes, but getting a transcript of the testimony isn't exactly easy, especially for a civilian who has no connection to the case."

"And you can't use Mike's name, because that'd get him mixed up in it and you don't want that."

"I certainly don't," Phyllis said. "He took a big enough chance just talking to me about the case. Sheriff Haney has been,

31

well, *tolerant* of me getting involved in certain cases, but there's no point in pushing my luck. Or Mike's luck."

"Well, then, it looks like you may have to tell Mike that you can't do anything for his friend after all. Seems like it's sorta out of your hands."

"Maybe." Phyllis frowned in thought. "I haven't made up my mind completely yet. I think I'm going to have to sleep on it."

"That's usually a good idea. Don't know how well you'll sleep with no air conditionin', though."

"Luckily, we have fans, and it'll be cooler by morning. I grew up sleeping with no air conditioner going, even in the hottest part of the summer."

"So did I, but you get used to bein' comfortable."

"That's true." She was very comfortable with most parts of her life, Phyllis mused, but sooner or later things were going to change. She might not like it, but it was inevitable.

So it only made sense to enjoy life as long as she could, she thought with a smile as she reached up and patted Sam's hand where it rested on her shoulder.

"What's this?" Carolyn asked as she came

into the kitchen the next morning and found Phyllis working at the counter.

"Gluten-free oatmeal muffins in a cup," Phyllis said. "Just an idea I came up with. I thought I might put it in the magazine."

For a while now, she had been writing a monthly column for the magazine *A Taste of Texas,* which had been a favorite publication of hers and Carolyn's for a long time. They had entered many of the magazine's recipe contests without winning, but they still enjoyed the friendly competition.

Then Phyllis had not only won, but the editor had also offered her the job of writing a column. That had been fun, although occasionally she got a little nervous about the deadlines.

If Carolyn resented Phyllis's success, she hadn't displayed it. Of course, it probably helped that Phyllis had showcased a few of Carolyn's recipes, always giving her full credit for them.

"You just mix oatmeal, egg, oil, and milk in a large cup and then microwave it. You can throw in some chocolate or fruit or nuts and make a quick breakfast that's not just plain. I've got some blueberries and cream cheese in these and sweetened it with maple syrup."

Sam had come into the kitchen in time to

hear the tail end of the conversation. He grinned and said, "I'm not sure what you're talkin' about, but it sure sounds good. And that coffee smells mighty good." He poured himself a cup. "Drinkin' hot coffee while the A/C's out and the house is warm. That's Texas for you. Never too cold for iced tea or too hot for coffee."

"You're just addicted to caffeine," Carolyn said as she poured a cup as well. "And don't make some crack about the pot calling the kettle black. I never claimed *not* to be addicted to caffeine. How can you teach school for all those years and not be?"

Sam had on a pair of blue jeans this morning, as well as shoes and socks. His t-shirt was a Poolville High School shirt, where he had taught and coached for many years. Carolyn wore a lightweight housedress while Phyllis was in capris again, although she wore a t-shirt, too, instead of a short-sleeved blouse like the day before.

There was room in the big microwave for all three cups of the oatmeal she had prepared. She placed them on the turntable, closed the door, and pushed buttons to start them cooking. She'd already had part of a cup of coffee. She picked it up from the counter and went to join Sam and Carolyn at the table.

As she sat down, the cell phone in her pocket began to ring. As she reached for the phone, she tried to remember the last time the landline had rung when it *wasn't* a telemarketer or some sort of survey.

"A little early for someone to be calling, isn't it?" Carolyn said.

"I hope it's not the air conditionin' guy cancellin'," Sam said.

"It's not," Phyllis told them. "It's Jimmy D'Angelo."

That bit of news caused Sam's bushy eyebrows to rise. Carolyn frowned and said, "That lawyer?"

Phyllis didn't respond to that. Instead she thumbed the icon on the screen and said, "Hello?"

She heard D'Angelo's familiar accent on the other end of the connection. He had grown up, attended law school, and started his career as an attorney somewhere in the Northeast. Phyllis hadn't asked him for any details about that or how he had come to be practicing law in Texas. In a couple of the cases in which Phyllis had become involved, D'Angelo had represented suspects charged with murder, suspects Phyllis had eventually proven to be innocent. In the course of those investigations, the attorney had asked Phyllis and Sam to work as consultants for him. Sam liked to joke that that made them private eyes. Phyllis didn't think so, at least not legally, but helping D'Angelo did give them some official standing and opened a few doors that might otherwise have remained closed.

She listened to D'Angelo now and said, "Yes, as a matter of fact, I *am* familiar with it" and "How did you —" and "We were about to sit down to breakfast" and "Yes, I suppose we could. When?" She nodded, even though the lawyer couldn't see that, and went on, "Yes, of course."

Then she hung up and looked at Carolyn and Sam. Carolyn said, "What in the world was that all about?"

Instead of answering directly, Phyllis said, "You were going to be here this morning, weren't you?"

"Actually, I plan to be here all day."

"Do you mind letting the air conditioner man in when he gets here?"

"No, but where are you and Sam going to be?"

Sam said, "I've got a hunch, but it sounds sorta crazy."

"Maybe not," Phyllis said. "Mr. D'Angelo wants to talk to both of us, Sam — about Roxanne Jackson's murder."

The microwave dinged to signal that it was done.

CHAPTER 4

Jimmy D'Angelo had said it would be fine for Phyllis and Sam to come to his office just off Weatherford's downtown square later that morning, so they were able to enjoy their breakfast. Sam proclaimed the oatmeal muffins in a cup delicious, as were all of Phyllis's recipes, according to him.

"I think we should change clothes before we go see Mr. D'Angelo," Phyllis said.

"What's wrong with the way we're dressed?" Sam asked. "I've got on shoes."

"Going to a law office requires a certain degree of professionalism."

"Tell that to some of the folks I've seen goin' in and out of that office. Anyway, we're not goin' to *court* — I hope."

"No, he just wants to talk to us. He didn't come right out and say so, but I got the feeling he's been hired to handle the appeal of Danny Jackson's conviction."

Carolyn took a sip of coffee, cocked an

eyebrow, and said, "I'm sure *that* is just a complete coincidence."

Phyllis knew what she meant by that. Under the circumstances, it was hard to believe anything other than that Mike had recommended D'Angelo to his old friend. Whether he had done it simply because Danny had asked him for the name of a good lawyer, or because Mike thought his mother would be more likely to get involved in the case that way, Phyllis couldn't say, and she supposed it didn't really matter.

"Well, I'm going to put on nicer clothes," she said. "You do what you want to, Sam."

"If you're willin' to be seen with me, I reckon it wouldn't hurt to clean up a little," he said. "You weren't talkin' about me puttin' on a *tie,* though, were you?"

"Heavens, no," Phyllis said.

Sam kept the blue jeans but put on a nice sports shirt. Phyllis changed to slacks and a blouse and sandals. They took her Lincoln. The square was only a few blocks away, but it was already warm enough outside that walking that far would be uncomfortable.

Parking around the square could be a challenge, and it took several minutes to find a place. It was almost ten o'clock before they walked into the offices of Harvick, Webber, and Crane, the firm where Jimmy

D'Angelo was an associate. The attractive blond receptionist knew them by now, so she gave them a smile and a friendly greeting and took them right to D'Angelo's office.

The lawyer stood up from the leather swivel chair behind his paper-littered desk and smiled, too, as he said, "Come in, come in. Good to see you again. It's been a while."

"We've been stayin' outta trouble," Sam said dryly. "Haven't needed a lawyer."

"Well, I'm glad there aren't more people who can say that, or I might be out of business. How are you, Mrs. Newsom?"

"I'm fine," Phyllis said. "What about you, Mr. D'Angelo?"

"Staying busy, thank goodness. Have a seat."

Two comfortable armchairs stood in front of the desk. Phyllis and Sam sat down, Sam hesitating just slightly so Phyllis would be seated first.

D'Angelo resumed his seat and clasped his hands together in front of him. His fingers were short and on the pudgy side, like the rest of him. His broad face had a permanent flush that showed he had a fondness for too much rich food and liquor. Phyllis knew perfectly well that she had a tendency to be a little judgmental sometimes, so she always suppressed the impulse to urge him to take better care of himself. She doubted if it would do any good, anyway.

"So," D'Angelo said. "Danny Jackson. I understand that you're acquainted with him."

"I've known Danny for more than twenty years," Phyllis said. "He and my son Mike have been friends since they were in junior high together."

"I never met the young fella myself," Sam said. "I've heard a lot about him, though."

"I got a call from him yesterday afternoon. I went over to Fort Worth to see him, and he asked me to handle his appeal."

That confirmed Phyllis's hunch. She said, "Have you taken the case?"

"To be honest with you, I haven't made up my mind yet. Murder cases are a real challenge, and I like a challenge. They can be good publicity, too. But they can get awfully ugly." D'Angelo shrugged. "I got a feeling this one might. But I'm interested enough I decided to do two things. One of 'em is talking to you."

"I'm sure Mike gave Danny your name, if that's what you're wondering about," Phyllis said. "He knows we worked with you on those other cases."

"And he wants you to help his friend, right?" D'Angelo said. "I'm guessing here, but that makes sense to me."

Phyllis nodded and said, "He came to see me and talked to me about Danny yesterday afternoon. He's convinced that Danny didn't kill his wife."

"You said you'd done two things," Sam put in. "What's the second one?"

D'Angelo tapped a blunt fingertip on a stack of papers on his desk and said, "I got a copy of the trial transcript faxed over from the Tarrant County DA's office. Care to take a look through it, Mrs. Newsom?"

Phyllis hadn't been able to stop herself from leaning forward slightly when D'Angelo mentioned the transcript. She knew he could tell she was eager to find out what it contained, so there was no point in denying that.

"Yes, I'd like to."

D'Angelo pushed the papers toward her.

"Why don't you take it in the conference room and look through it?" he suggested. "I have a few other things to take care of this morning. We can talk when you've finished with it."

"All right," Phyllis said.

They knew where the conference room was from their previous visits to the office.

42

Phyllis gathered up the transcript, which made a surprisingly thin sheaf of papers. But then, from what she'd read and been told, the trial had been short and simple.

The conference room was behind massive oak double doors. Inside was a long, gleaming hardwood table with heavy wooden chairs around it. The walls were dark wood, decorated with framed portraits of the firm's partners and some landscapes. The thick carpet helped muffle sound and gave the big room a hushed atmosphere, almost like a church.

Phyllis and Sam sat down side by side at the table. Phyllis began reading the transcript, passing each sheet to Sam as she finished it. She valued his opinion about these cases, and sometimes he spotted things that she had missed.

Trial transcripts made for pretty dull reading, she discovered. There was a lot of what amounted to boilerplate at the beginning: jury selection, reading of the charge, opening statements.

Then came the meat of what she was looking for — the testimony of the witnesses called by the prosecution, beginning with the Fort Worth police officer who had responded to Danny Jackson's 911 call about finding his wife bloody and unresponsive.

Danny had been cooperative, but in a shocked, disoriented state. An ambulance had arrived within minutes of the officer, and the EMTs had quickly determined that Roxanne Jackson was dead on the scene. Homicide detectives had been summoned, along with a forensics unit. Danny was isolated within the building from the crime scene and held for questioning.

That interrogation had established Roxanne and Danny's identities, where they worked, and where they had been that day. Phyllis had already heard Danny's story, and reading the transcript confirmed that it had been reported accurately in the newspaper.

But examination of the shop's front and rear doors showed no signs of breaking and entering. A call to the shop's owner had established that the doors should have been locked. Roxanne had been working on restocking the hair care products the salon sold, and the shop was closed for the day. This immediately cast doubts on Danny's speculation — which he had voiced to the detectives — about Roxanne interrupting a burglary. It appeared that she must have let the killer in, which would indicate she knew

44

him. The woman who had gotten a license to carry a handgun because she was nervous about leaving work late wouldn't have unlocked the door for a stranger.

The medical examiner had testified that Roxanne had no defensive wounds on her hands. Her jaw was broken on the left side, leading him to theorize that Roxanne's assailant was right-handed — like Danny — and had struck her there first, with enough force to render her unconscious, then carried out the rest of the beating that had taken her life. That explained the lack of defensive wounds.

She'd never had a chance to fight back.

And the knuckles of Danny Jackson's right hand were skinned and bruised.

"Well, it's not hard to see why they thought Danny was guilty," Phyllis commented as she paused in her reading.

Sam nodded and pointed at the sheet of paper he was holding.

"It's a pretty plausible scenario. No signs of a break-in. Evidence that indicates she knew her attacker, otherwise she wouldn't have let him get close enough to knock her out like that. Wounds on Danny's hand that looked like he'd been beatin' on something, not to mention him bein' covered with her blood. Shoot, I probably would have ar-

45

rested him, too."

"And no alibi," Phyllis said. "Also, the detectives talked to everyone who worked around there, and no one saw any strangers hanging around the salon or the shopping center where it's located."

"Nobody saw much of anything," Sam said. "We'll have to take a look at the place ourselves, though. Maybe the cops overlooked somebody."

"You're assuming we're going to get involved in this."

Sam shrugged and said, "Sure. But I'm curious to see what Danny had to say for himself."

"So am I," Phyllis said.

Danny's defense attorney had cross-examined each of the witnesses as the prosecution's case went on, but he couldn't shake them from their testimony that there was nothing to indicate a burglary. The medical evidence was strong, too, although the lawyer had gotten the medical examiner to admit that he couldn't be *sure* the blow to the jaw had been struck first and had indeed rendered Roxanne unconscious.

"But the fact that there were no defensive wounds on the victim's hands or anywhere else is indisputable," the ME had testified. "In my professional opinion, that indicates the initial blow — whichever one it was — knocked her out so she couldn't fight back. And then the attacker methodically went on to beat her to death."

The defense had objected to that last sentence as inflammatory and prejudicial and the judge had ordered it stricken, but the damage, of course, had already been done.

Other testimony had addressed the question of motive. Two of Roxanne's co-workers at Paul's Beauty Salon had testified they had heard and seen Roxanne and Danny arguing on several occasions when Danny had come by the salon. The issue seemed to be finances, as it often was when couples clashed. Danny and Roxanne had put quite a bit of money into buying the old farm property and remodeling the house, and even though she had a steady job, the business in which he was a partner ate up most of those profits. So for the most part, they were living on what she made, and her friends at the salon said she had resented that.

"So they were arguin'," Sam said, "and it got outta hand."

"That's certainly how the prosecution made it sound," Phyllis agreed. "And of course, it could have easily happened just that way."

"Yep. Mike doesn't believe it, though."

Phyllis went back to the transcript. The prosecution had rested its case. Danny's attorney hadn't mounted much of a defense. A couple of Danny's friends and his business partner, Brian Flynn, had testified that he was a great guy and was devoted to Roxanne and would never hurt her. But under cross-examination by the prosecution, even they had admitted that the couple had argued in the past.

To cap things off, Danny had taken the stand in his own defense, telling his version of what had happened that terrible evening in what came across, even in the printed transcript, as a calm, steady voice. But there had been more hesitation the farther he went in the story, and Phyllis could almost see him there in the witness chair, his voice breaking slightly as the strain deepened on his face.

When asked about the wounds on his hand, he had explained that he'd banged it up when a fender he was working on had fallen on it. That seemed reasonable enough, but there was no way to prove it because it had happened after his partner left the shop that day. When pressed on cross-examination about the arguments, he'd had no choice but to admit that he and Roxanne had had a few fights about money.

"Like any married couple that's struggling to get ahead," he had declared. "With the economy the way it is now and just getting worse all the time, not that many people our age even *try* anymore. Of course we fussed at each other some. That doesn't mean I didn't love her or that I would . . . that I would . . ."

Danny hadn't been able to go on. His emotions had gotten the better of him. But of course the prosecutor had implied that was just an act to get the jury to feel sorry for him.

If that was true, it hadn't worked. Less than an hour after both sides had rested, made their closing statements, and the judge had given his instructions to the jury, those twelve peers had been back with a verdict of guilty on one count of second-degree murder. The next day, that same jury had sentenced Danny to thirty years in prison . . . a sentence he would start serving at the penitentiary in Huntsville as soon as the paperwork got straightened out.

Phyllis handed the last page of the transcript to Sam. It took him only a moment to read it, turn it over, and add it to the stack of papers he'd made in front of him.

"Who's goin' first?" he asked.

"You can," Phyllis said.

"There's nothing that jumps out at me. Looks like the cops made a good, solid case. Not air-tight, mind you. There aren't any eyewitnesses, and there's not a lot of physical evidence. But what is there points to Danny." Sam tapped the stack of papers. "From the looks of this, his lawyer didn't do much to help him, but he didn't foul up anything, either."

Phyllis nodded slowly and said, "That's the way I see it, too. But there's no indication that anyone — either the sheriff's department investigator or Danny's attorney — looked into the question of who *else* might have had a reason for wanting Roxanne dead. They also didn't check for Danny's blood on the bumper to see if his story was true."

Sam frowned and thought about that, then said, "Everybody just went with the conventional wisdom that the spouse is always the prime suspect. What evidence there was, matched up with Danny just fine, so that was that. Can't blame 'em too much. There's a reason something becomes conventional wisdom."

"Because it's usually right," Phyllis said. "But not always."

"Nope," Sam said. "Not always."

"And there's something else . . ."

Sam leaned toward her and asked, "You got an idea?"

"No, it's not clear enough in my head to call it an idea. It's more just a . . . sense . . . that something's not right, that the facts don't match up quite as neatly as they appear to at first glance."

"That's enough for me," Sam said with an emphatic nod. "If you've got doubts that Danny's guilty, we got to look into it."

"I think you're right." Phyllis pushed back the heavy chair. "Let's go talk to Mr. D'Angelo."

CHAPTER 5

"I'll let Mr. Jackson know I'm going to take his case, and I'll file an appeal immediately," Jimmy D'Angelo said as he sat back in his chair, laced his fingers together on his ample belly, and grinned at Phyllis and Sam. "I'll also file a motion requesting that he continues to be held in custody in the Tarrant County jail rather than transferred to TDC in Huntsville."

"Will that be better?" Phyllis asked.

"County's no bed and breakfast," D'Angelo said with a shrug, "but I'd rather have him close by. It's a legitimate request since I'll need to confer with my client . . . and so will my investigators."

He pointed both forefingers across the desk at Phyllis and Sam, with his thumbs raised to make them look like guns.

"That still seems strange to me," Phyllis said. "We have absolutely no qualifications to be investigators."

"Other than solving a dozen murders." D'Angelo chuckled. "All right, I'll get the wheels in motion." He made a shooing motion with his hands. "Go do what you do. Just let me know how it's going. I'll go over to Fort Worth and talk to Danny and try to be encouraging."

As they left the office, Sam said, "Mike's gonna be happy. Or at least, maybe not quite as worried about his old friend. I don't reckon he'll be happy until Danny is cleared."

"Things could still turn out badly," Phyllis reminded him. "Mr. D'Angelo won't be able to get Danny's conviction set aside without strong evidence that he's not guilty. That's going to require discovering who *did* kill Roxanne. Reasonable doubt won't be enough."

"So we'll find the real killer," Sam said confidently.

"And hope that it doesn't turn out to be Danny himself."

"Yeah, there's that," Sam admitted.

Phyllis wasn't sure of Mike's work schedule, so she didn't want to call his cell phone to let him know she was going to look into the case. She might wake him. She would call Sarah a little later, she decided, and ask her to have Mike call back when it was convenient for him.

As Phyllis pulled the Lincoln into the driveway back home, the first thing she noticed was that the front door was closed. They had been leaving the wooden door open and hooking the screen door while the central unit wasn't working so that air would circulate better through the house. The sight of the closed door raised her hopes, and as she and Sam walked through the garage entrance into the kitchen, she felt cool air blowing from the vents in the ceiling.

A big grin appeared on Sam's face as he said, "Doesn't that feel nice?"

Carolyn came down the hall from the living room to meet them. She waved a hand and said, "I guess you can tell the air conditioning man has been here."

"He got it fixed that quickly?" Phyllis said.

"He just had to replace two little parts. A solarnoid and a capacitater, I think he called them."

"You mean a solenoid and a capacitor," Sam said.

"Isn't that what I said?" Carolyn responded with a glare.

A quick glance from Phyllis told Sam he would be wise not to pursue this line of conversation. He smiled and nodded and said, "Well, I'm sure glad it's fixed, that's all I got to say."

"So am I," Phyllis said. "Is he going to send me a bill?"

"That's right. I would have paid him myself, but you said to do it the other way." Carolyn paused. "How did it go at the lawyer's office?"

"Interesting," Phyllis said.

Carolyn gave her a look. "You're going to investigate that poor young woman's murder, aren't you?"

"I want to see justice done," Phyllis said, "and I have a feeling that so far, maybe it hasn't been."

Carolyn had already started lunch, bacon tomato pie, along with a spinach salad that included chunks of pear, bleu cheese crumbles, walnuts, and a refreshing lime dressing.

As they sat down to eat before Phyllis and Sam pondered their next move in the case, Carolyn said, "I've been thinking about that magazine you work for, Phyllis."

"*A Taste of Texas?* What about it?"

"Well, you know, I haven't entered any of their recipe contests since you started writing your column."

Phyllis thought about it and realized her

friend was right. If Carolyn had come up with a recipe she liked well enough to enter in a contest, she would have said something about it, and she hadn't.

"I'm sorry," Phyllis said instantly, feeling a bit guilty because she *hadn't* noticed. "You haven't stopped entering because of me, have you?"

"Well, I thought it would look bad and probably wouldn't even be allowed. You know, all sorts of contests and sweepstakes have fine print about how employees of the company sponsoring them, and even relatives of employees, are prohibited from entering. I think it may even be a law."

Phyllis shook her head and said, "I don't think it's a law. More like a policy. And we're not related."

"I know that, of course. But we're friends, and for goodness' sake, I live in your house. If I entered a contest and won, and the connection between us got back to the magazine, we might both get in trouble."

"My editor knows you and I are friends," Phyllis pointed out. "I've mentioned you several times in the column and used some of your recipes."

"I know, and I appreciate that. But I miss the competition. I like the feeling of sending something in and hoping that I might *win.*"

Phyllis could understand that. For a long time, she had entered her recipes in various contests, and it was always exciting. The thrill of competition, they called it, and there was a lot of truth to that old saying.

"After lunch — which is delicious, by the way — I'll get one of the issues of the magazine and look at it. I really don't think you should have to give up entering their contests because of me."

"Neither do I," Sam said. "And this tomato pie is mighty good, by the way. I like how you can put two things together you don't normally think of that way, and it turns out to taste great."

"Fusion," Carolyn said. "Although this is a rather down to earth version of it."

"Whatever you call it, I like it."

The most recent issue of *A Taste of Texas* was in the living room. After cleaning up the lunch dishes, Phyllis found it and turned to the pages containing information about the current contest, which was looking for fruit pie recipes. She couldn't find anything about friends of the magazine's employees being prohibited from entering, or even relatives of employees.

She pointed that out to Carolyn and said, "I promise you, I'm just a tiny fish in this pond. I couldn't pull any strings to help you win even if I wanted to."

"And you don't," Carolyn said.

"Of course not. We've both always competed fair and square."

"That's the only way winning means anything." Carolyn took another look at the magazine. "There's still a week until the deadline for sending in entries. I'd better get busy!"

"Do you have anything in mind?"

"As a matter of fact, I do," Carolyn said, but she didn't elaborate. She'd always been tight-lipped about recipes when she was working on them, and Phyllis knew she wasn't going to change at this late date.

When Carolyn had gone back into the kitchen, Sam joined Phyllis in the living room.

"Get it all squared away?" he asked.

"I think so. She's going to enter the current contest. I'm sorry she felt like she couldn't do that until now."

"You didn't know she'd stopped on account of you writin' for the magazine."

"That's just it. I should have known."

"Well, it's settled now," Sam said. "How do you reckon we ought to start on the other chore that we're lookin' at?"

Phyllis knew he was talking about investigating Roxanne Jackson's murder. She thought about it for a moment and then said, "I want to take a look at the crime scene."

Paul's Beauty Salon, located on Camp Bowie Boulevard in west Fort Worth, was about a thirty-minute drive away from Phyllis's house in Weatherford, and a significant part of that time was spent navigating through the traffic that clogged South Main Street where it crossed Interstate 20. Phyllis remembered quite well when there hadn't been anything past Tin Top Road except a pleasant drive through the country to Granbury, but huge shopping centers and tons of traffic were part of the price of progress, she supposed.

Although sometimes she wondered if maybe that price was a little too high.

But by two o'clock in the afternoon, she and Sam were on Camp Bowie, this time in Sam's pickup with him at the wheel, as they looked for the beauty salon where Roxanne Jackson had been killed. Phyllis had looked up the address before they left and programmed it into the GPS app on her phone, even though Sam had assured her he could find the place. He really was a bit of a "livin', breathin' GPS", as he sometimes claimed, but he wasn't infallible.

Camp Bowie Boulevard was named for the Army camp established on the west side of Fort Worth during World War I, Phyllis knew. It had been a sprawling base covering much of the area where the Botanic Gardens were now located, and its establishment had sparked a housing boom that had extended the town for miles in that direction. A lot of wealthy people had flocked to the area, and many of those old-money families still lived on the west side. The boulevard wasn't as ritzy as it once had been — nowhere was, Phyllis thought — but there were still quite a few stretches of high-end establishments that catered to the wealthy.

Paul's Beauty Salon was located in one of those shopping centers, although it was in its own brick building at one end of the center. The nearest business was an expensive dress shop, flanked on the other side by a jewelry store. All the businesses shared the same parking lot, and there were quite a few cars in it this afternoon, mostly luxury sedans but also a few crossovers and SUVs.

"We didn't think this through," Sam said as he pulled into the parking lot. "This ol' pickup of mine is gonna stand out like the proverbial sore thumb. We should've brought your car."

"That's all right. I don't much like driving in a lot of traffic anymore. If people want to be snooty and look down their noses at your pickup, let them go ahead and do it. It doesn't mean anything to me except that they're stuck-up, and that's *their* problem."

"That's sorta the way I feel about it," Sam said with a smile. He parked between a Lexus and a Cadillac Escalade. "Do you want me to come in with you or stay out here?"

Phyllis thought about it for a moment, then said, "Why don't you stay out here, if you don't mind? I'm going to try to get an appointment to have my hair done, so right now all I'll be doing is glancing around the place, just to get it in my head so I can see if everything matches up with the transcript we read."

"Fine with me. I'll have a look around the shoppin' center, see if there's anything that strikes me as funny."

Phyllis nodded and said, "That's a good idea. We'll meet back here."

"This isn't the sort of place where you can just walk in and they'll take care of you right away, though, is it?"

"I doubt it. But I'll see how long it'll be before I can make an appointment."

"And while they're doin' your hair, you

can do a little gossipin' about the murder that took place here, right?"

"That's the idea," Phyllis said. She got out of the pickup and walked toward the building.

CHAPTER 6

Phyllis had been in many beauty shops over the years, and to one extent or another, they all smelled the same, similar to chemical factories, with pungent fumes. The combination of excessive heat from all the hair dryers with chemicals used in hair dyes, hair straightening, permanent waves, and hairsprays created some interesting fumes. Paul's Beauty Salon, being the upscale establishment it was, was obviously well ventilated and tried to mask that distinctive mixture of chemical scents with a pleasant peppermint aroma, but to Phyllis, as soon as she stepped into the place it still smelled like a beauty shop.

The heavy wooden door with a double layer of stained glass slowly swung shut behind her. The floor was brilliantly polished wood as well. The lighting in the entrance foyer was subdued, although Phyllis could see through double glass doors into a much larger and better lit area where the beauticians' chairs, wash stands, and hair dryers were arranged around the room. To Phyllis's right in the reception area were a comfortable-looking leather loveseat and a pair of matching armchairs. To the left was a desk with a computer on it and a young woman with blue and purple hair behind it.

She wore a small, floppy-brimmed hat that looked Sixties vintage to Phyllis. The hair on the left side of her head was blue, long, and straight, and hung down over her shoulder. The purple hair on the right side of her head was done in tightly braided corn rows. Her left nostril was pierced and had a tiny stud in it. A tattoo of some sort serpentined down her bare, muscular right arm. Despite all those things, which just looked *odd* to Phyllis, the young woman had a pretty face, beautiful brown eyes, and a friendly smile as she looked up from the computer monitor and said, "Hello. Can I help you?"

"Yes, I've heard wonderful things about this salon and was hoping I could make an appointment to have my hair styled."

"Of course." A look of concern appeared on the young woman's face. "But I'm afraid we're booked solid for the next two weeks."

Phyllis's glance through the double glass

doors had told her the salon was busy, with clients at most of the stations. Being the scene of a murder might have hurt business for a while, but that crime had taken place long enough ago that the effect had worn off. Anyway, as morbid as most people were these days, it was entirely possible the grisly notoriety might have been *good* for business.

"I can put you on our cancellation list if you'd like," the receptionist went on.

"That would be very nice, dear."

The young woman tapped a few keys on the computer and asked, "What's that name?"

"Phyllis Newsom." Phyllis wasn't the sort to go incognito. Keeping up with a false identity would have been too much trouble, too difficult to remember.

"And the phone number?"

Phyllis gave the receptionist her cell phone number.

"We'll give you a call right away if something opens up. My name is Aurora, by the way."

"Why, that's a lovely name."

"Thanks." She grinned. "It's kind of a hippy-dippy name, I know, but you can blame my grandma for it. My grandparents were hippies, I guess. Grandma insisted my parents call me Aurora. She said the name came to her in a vision from another spiritual plane." Aurora lowered her voice to a conspiratorial tone. "I think she may have been dropping some acid back then, though."

This conversation was starting to make Phyllis feel old. Her own grandson was still a pre-schooler, and yet this young woman with her multi-colored hair was the granddaughter of someone who had to be roughly the same age as Phyllis.

"You said you'd heard good things about the salon," Aurora went on. "Do you mind me asking who told you about us?"

Phyllis didn't have an answer ready for that question. She said, "Oh, goodness, I don't really remember, one of my friends who lives over here, it must have been. This has been a while back." She paused. "But I do recall her mentioning that her favorite stylist was named Roxanne. If it would be possible to have her take care of me . . ."

Phyllis knew that mentioning Roxanne's name was a bit of a risk, but she thought she could chance it, as friendly and innocuous as the conversation had been so far.

Aurora's smile disappeared instantly, though. Her tone was professionally polite and nothing more as she said, "I'm afraid

66

that won't be possible. Roxanne doesn't work here anymore."

"Did she go to another salon? My friend was really fond of her."

"I thought you said you couldn't remember which friend recommended us."

"Well, I'm not sure —"

Aurora cut her off with a curt head shake. "It doesn't matter. Roxanne is dead."

Phyllis opened her eyes wider and tried to look shocked. She said, "Oh, I'm so sorry. I had no idea. I don't know what happened, but I'm sorry if I upset you by mentioning your friend —"

Aurora interrupted her again by saying, "Roxanne wasn't my friend. She just worked here. Anyway, it was a while back. If anybody was upset, they're over it by now."

The way she phrased it made it sound as if Roxanne's murder hadn't really bothered anyone at Paul's Beauty Salon, Phyllis thought. There hadn't been anything in what she had read to indicate that Roxanne wasn't well-liked at the salon, but if that was true, it made things a bit more interesting. *Someone* must have had a good reason for killing Roxanne, and if it wasn't Danny, the next most likely suspects were the people she worked with.

"So, I've got your name on the cancellation list," Aurora went on briskly. "If there's nothing else I can do for you . . ."

Phyllis knew she was being dismissed. She didn't like the feeling, especially when it came from someone so much younger than her. She controlled that reaction, though, and said, "Really, again, I'm sorry —"

Aurora stood up, revealing that she was a couple of inches taller than Phyllis. The jeans she wore, fashionably snug and torn at the knees, and her t-shirt hugged the trim body of an athlete. The muscles in her arms showed that she worked out. She said, "It's all right. I have to go —"

Phyllis wasn't sure where she was going, since her job was to sit at this reception desk, but before either of them could do anything else, one of the glass doors swung open and a woman stepped into the foyer.

"Anything wrong out here, Aurora?" she asked.

The newcomer was in her forties, maybe close to fifty, Phyllis estimated, but still attractive with fluffy red hair cut fairly short around her head. Unlike the stylists, who were younger and wore snug black pants under their salon smocks, this woman had on a nice black dress, nylons, and sensible heels. Her voice had an unmistakable Southern accent, much more Georgia or Alabama than Texas.

"No, Pauline, it's fine," Aurora answered. "I was just adding this lady's name to the cancellation list."

The redhead smiled at Phyllis and said, "I don't recall seeing you in here before."

"First time," Phyllis said.

"A friend of hers recommended us to her, but she doesn't remember who," Aurora said, making the comment sound vaguely accusatory.

"Well, I'm not surprised, we have so many ladies coming through here," the redhead said. She held out her hand to Phyllis. "I'm Pauline Gibbs. This is my salon."

Phyllis took the woman's hand and said, "Phyllis Newsom. There's no Paul of Paul's Beauty Salon?"

Pauline Gibbs laughed and shook her head.

"No, I'm afraid poor ol' Paul is a figment of my imagination. Some ladies like the idea of a male stylist. All the superstars in the field are men, you know. Startin' out, I used to pretend that there really was a Paul and he owned the place, but as our clients came to know and trust us and rely on us, I gradually dropped that fiction. There wasn't really any need for it." She changed the subject by continuing, "I hope Aurora here took good care of you, Phyllis."

Clearly, she was one of those women who was on a first-name basis with everybody right away.

"She certainly did," Phyllis replied. Aurora still stood there, arms crossed over her chest now, not actually glaring but looking none too friendly. Phyllis thought about letting things go for the moment, but instinct told her to push just a little more. "I'm afraid I upset her, though."

"Oh?" Pauline arched perfectly plucked eyebrows. "How did you manage to do that?"

"She asked about Roxanne," Aurora said.

Pauline looked surprised. Phyllis said quickly, "I only asked about her because my friend was fond of the way this Roxanne did her hair. I had no idea there had been a . . . a tragedy of some sort."

There, she thought. That made it sound like she didn't know what had happened to Roxanne.

"Well, I'm sure you didn't mean anything by it," Pauline said. "You understand how it is, though . . . You work with somebody and something terrible happens to them, it's a little hard to forget about it and move on." She paused. "We've done the best we can, though."

70

"Of course. I won't take up any more of your time. I can see that you're awfully busy . . ." Phyllis gestured vaguely toward the salon's main room.

"Did you make an appointment for later on, in case nothing comes up sooner?"

"No, actually, I forgot."

"Take care of that, would you, Aurora?" Pauline said. It was phrased as a request and the redhead's voice was still honeysuckle and magnolias, but Phyllis thought she heard some underlying steel in Pauline's tone. The way Aurora scuttled back behind the desk and started tapping on the keyboard told Phyllis that Pauline was accustomed to quick responses from her employees.

"How about . . . two weeks from next Wednesday at one o'clock?" Aurora asked without looking up.

"That'll be fine," Phyllis said. She didn't know if she would keep the appointment or not. For one thing, she hadn't asked what the prices were here. But it wouldn't hurt to have the appointment. She could always cancel it later.

Aurora wrote the date and time on a reminder card and handed it to her. Phyllis thanked her, and Aurora managed to work up a perfunctory smile.

"We'll see you then, if not sooner," Pauline said brightly as Phyllis turned toward the outer door.

"Yes, thank you. Goodbye."

She stepped outside and saw that Sam was already in the pickup. He had his phone out and was looking at it. Probably checking his e-mail or maybe reading one of his old Western novels, she thought, knowing that he had an e-reader app on the phone. He still preferred the scent of decomposing paper and dust, as he put it whenever he inhaled the aroma of a 50-year-old paperback, but being able to read on the phone sometimes came in handy, too.

"Find out anything?" Phyllis asked as she climbed into the passenger seat and closed the door.

"Just that the stores around here are on the fancy side," Sam said. "Most of 'em seem aimed at the ladies, but there's a menswear joint down at the other end of the shoppin' center. I went in there and pretended to be lookin' for a new suit. They were eager to help me out, but the fellas I talked to didn't know anything about a murder down here at the beauty shop. One older man said he remembered it happenin', but that's all. The other two were younger guys and weren't even workin' there when

Roxanne was killed."

"You didn't buy a suit?" Phyllis asked with a smile.

Sam shook his head and said, "Nope. I've got a good funeral suit, in case I have to go to one that's formal enough to need it. These days, folks don't dress up for funerals like they once did." He paused. "Of course, when you get to be my age, you start thinkin' about makin' sure you've got a nice suit for your own funeral. Although jeans would work just as good as far as I'm concerned."

"You're not going to need that for a long time," Phyllis told him.

Sam's shrug was an eloquent way of saying *You never know.*

"How about you?" he asked.

"What do I want to wear to my own funeral, you mean?"

He laughed and shook his head.

"Actually, I was askin' if you found out anything there in the beauty shop."

"It's not really a beauty shop. It's a beauty salon. I'm surprised they don't have 'Spa' in the name. But I didn't find out much."

"Not much means you did come up with *something.*"

"I have an appointment for a couple of weeks from now," Phyllis said, "and they have my name and number in case there's a cancellation between now and then. I talked to the receptionist, and I also met the woman who owns the place."

"I thought it belonged to a fella named Paul."

"Pauline. Paul is just for name purposes." Phyllis went on to describe the conversation, then said, "I got the feeling that Roxanne wasn't necessarily well-liked, but to be fair, I only talked to the two of them. There were half a dozen other women working there, and I have no idea yet how they felt about her. One thing *did* occur to me, though."

"What's that?"

Phyllis thought about the muscles in Aurora's arms and how the young woman carried herself like an athlete. She said, "I've been assuming all along that a man killed Roxanne, I guess because she was beaten to death. It just never occurred to me that a woman could have done it. But I realize now I could be wrong about that. A woman might have been strong enough to have committed that murder."

"You got anybody in mind?"

"It's much too soon for that," Phyllis replied with a shake of her head. "But I certainly think I'm going to have to find out more about how Roxanne got along with the people she worked with. I can think of someone who might be able to tell us, and we were going to have to talk to him anyway."

"We're gonna go see Danny," Sam said.

Phyllis nodded and said, "That's exactly what we're going to do."

CHAPTER 7

Paying a visit to Danny Jackson in jail was going to take some arranging, and it was too late in the day to worry about that now, so Phyllis and Sam headed back to Weatherford. Along the way, Phyllis called Jimmy D'Angelo's office, told him what they needed, and he declared that he would get right on it and let them know when he had something set up.

"I never spent much time in beauty shops," Sam mused as he drove. "Vicky wasn't the sort who wanted me along. Anyway, I was at school most of the time. You know how there was almost always more to do than you had time for."

"I certainly do."

"Of course, I had to take her to have her hair done now and then after . . . well, after things got bad. She never stopped carin' about how she looked no matter how rotten she felt."

Phyllis nodded. Sam's wife Vicky had passed away several years earlier, after a lengthy struggle against cancer. He spoke of her occasionally, and Phyllis knew him well enough by now to know that her death was still painful for him, although he had come to grips with it. She felt the same way about Kenny, although he had been gone longer than Vicky had. Neither of them brought up their former spouses that often, but they didn't try to avoid the subject, either. As with most things, it was just natural between them and nothing to be shied away from.

"Whenever I *did* find myself in a beauty shop," Sam went on, "it could be the ladies were a little more on guard since there was a man in their midst. I got the feelin', though, that if I hadn't been there, there wouldn't have been many holds barred in what they talked about."

Phyllis laughed and said, "Goodness gracious, no. There's something about that atmosphere that makes women say things they probably wouldn't in other surroundings."

"Gossip, in other words."

"Of course. But gossip implies that you're talking about somebody else. I've heard women admit things about themselves that would almost make your jaw drop. There aren't many secrets in a beauty shop, that's for sure."

"I reckon a fancy *salon* is the same way." Sam grinned. "Just a little more genteel."

"I wouldn't be a bit surprised," Phyllis said.

When they got home, Carolyn was preparing chicken stuffed jalapeño poppers for supper. While Sam went into the backyard to spend some time with Buck, Phyllis started putting together avocado salad to go with them. The two of them had worked together in this kitchen long enough that they knew instinctively how to stay out of each other's way.

"Did you find out anything?" Carolyn asked.

"Not really, not yet. But I haven't had a chance to talk to anyone where Roxanne worked except a couple of people." Phyllis summed up the visit to Paul's Beauty Salon, as she had for Sam earlier, concluding, "I plan to ask Danny how she got along with everyone else there."

Carolyn turned to look at her with something approaching horror on her face.

"You're going to see him?" she asked.

"That's right."

"In *jail*?"

With a faint smile, Phyllis said, "It won't

be the first time I've visited someone in jail, will it? In fact, if you recall, I've spent some time behind bars myself."

"Oh, I remember, all right. That whole thing was ridiculous. What was the district attorney thinking?"

"That I had concealed evidence and obstructed justice. Which I sort of had, I suppose. Not the obstructing justice part, though. I was trying to see that justice was done. That's true here, too."

"Yes, but Danny Jackson is a convicted murderer."

"Convicted, but possibly not guilty."

"In the eyes of the law, he is. But the main thing that concerns me is you'll be going over to Fort Worth to see him. Tarrant County isn't Parker County, Phyllis."

"Well, no. But Parker County isn't what it used to be, either. It's a lot more crowded than it used to be, and Mike says the crime is steadily getting worse. But I'll have Sam with me, and probably Mr. D'Angelo, too, so I don't think I have anything to worry about."

"An old man and a fat little lawyer. Yes, I'm sure they'll be able to handle anything that comes up."

Phyllis didn't see any point in continuing this line of discussion, so she changed the subject by saying, "How are you coming along with the recipe you're going to send in for the magazine contest?"

"It's getting there," Carolyn said. "I should have something for you to sample in another day or two."

"I'm looking forward to it. I don't suppose you want to give me a hint what it is?"

Carolyn smiled, shook her head, and said, "No, I don't."

That made Phyllis laugh, and murderers and jail visits were forgotten for the moment.

Jimmy D'Angelo called after supper.

"We're seeing Danny at 10:30 tomorrow morning," he said. "Just you and me, though. I'm afraid Sam won't be able to go along. Well, he can come with you, but he'll have to wait in the jail lobby."

"All right, if that's the way it has to be," Phyllis said, although she was disappointed by that part of D'Angelo's news. She always liked having Sam around, and sometimes he noticed things that she didn't. She had a good memory, though, and would fill him in on everything that was said after the interview with Danny Jackson.

"Just remember, carry as little metal as possible, and no weapons."

"Don't worry, I won't pack heat," Phyllis said with a laugh.

Metal detectors were everywhere these days. You couldn't go anywhere near government offices without having to go through one. Sam had had to go back to his pickup and leave his pocketknife there enough times that he had finally stopped carrying it, even though he was disgusted by that development. He'd had a knife in his pocket every day of his life since junior high, he had said, and it just didn't seem right not carrying one. But he was so accustomed to it that he had completely forgotten about it those times he had tried to take it in somewhere it wasn't allowed.

"Nobody better gripe when they need a box cut open and I don't have a pocketknife, though," he had said. "It's not my fault."

After saying goodbye to D'Angelo, Phyllis went into the living room to find Sam and tell him what the attorney had arranged.

"I don't like it much," he said with a slight frown. "I'd rather go in there with you. But if they won't allow more than two visitors at a time, I don't suppose there's much we can do about it."

From the sofa on the other side of the room, Carolyn sniffed and said, "Just hope there's not a riot."

"I always do," Sam said solemnly.

They were supposed to meet Jimmy D'Angelo at the Tarrant County jail at ten o'clock the next morning. The jail was located on Belknap Street at the northern edge of downtown Fort Worth, on a bluff overlooking the winding course of the Trinity River. Phyllis had never been in the jail before, but she recalled parking not far from here in a vast lot beside the river, then riding the Leonards' Department Store M&O Subway — the world's only privately owned subway system — into downtown for shopping excursions.

The subway was gone now, another victim of the constant change that had altered the face of downtown Fort Worth just as it had everywhere else. Though she'd heard rumors that the tunnel still existed, down there in the bluff on which the city sat. That was a creepy enough thought to make shivers go down a person's back.

Sam remembered the subway, too, and lamented its passing. He said, "Sure was easier to park down there in the Leonards' parkin' lot than to fight the traffic up here in town."

He found an empty meter on a side street that sloped down fairly sharply toward the river and fed enough quarters in it to keep them safely parked there for a couple of hours. The two of them walked up the slanting sidewalk, turned the corner onto Belknap, and headed for the jail a block away.

Most of the men and women going in and out of the tall building were neatly dressed in professional attire. Lawyers, Phyllis thought. The ones in jeans, like her and Sam, were probably here to visit prisoners.

D'Angelo was waiting for them just inside the lobby, holding his briefcase in his right hand and using his left to hold his phone as he talked. He nodded to Phyllis and Sam to indicate that he saw them as he finished up his conversation. Then he slipped the phone back into his pocket and said, "Right on time. There's been a little delay, though."

"Something wrong?" Phyllis asked.

"I'm not sure. They'll let us know when we can talk to Danny. In the meantime, let's sit down and you can tell me what you've found out so far."

Phyllis shook her head and said, "Nothing that's going to help very much, I'm afraid."

"Maybe you've found something but just don't know what it means yet."

"I don't think we can count on that."

The three of them sat down on a plastic

83

bench with Phyllis in the middle. She explained how she had visited Paul's Beauty Salon the day before.

"Going undercover," D'Angelo said with a nod. "I like it."

It didn't take long for Phyllis to give him the details of the conversation she'd had with Aurora and Pauline Gibbs.

"Sounds like this Aurora girl didn't get along that well with Roxanne," the lawyer commented. "Might be something there."

"Or everything she said might be totally innocent," Phyllis pointed out. "I'm hoping Danny can tell us more about that, and anything else that went on between Roxanne and the other women who worked there."

"Even if she didn't get along with some of them, that won't be enough to overturn Danny's conviction or even get him a new trial. We'll have to have proof of who really killed Roxanne."

Phyllis had made the same comment to Sam earlier, so she nodded.

"A confession would be nice, wouldn't it?"

"I'll settle for good solid evidence," D'Angelo said.

They had been sitting there for about forty-five minutes when a uniformed officer came over to them and said, "Mr. D'Angelo?

You and your associate can see your client now."

As Phyllis and D'Angelo stood up, Sam said, "I'll be waitin' right here."

They had to empty their pockets and go through two metal detectors before they reached the interview room where they would talk to Danny Jackson. D'Angelo had had to leave his briefcase and cell phone in a locked basket. He had only a legal pad and a couple of pens. Phyllis was empty-handed.

The room was spartanly furnished with a metal table and two metal chairs on each side of it. All were bolted to the floor. There was a mirror on one wall. Phyllis supposed it was one of those infamous two-way mirrors, although she couldn't be sure of that. She certainly wasn't going to wave at it. A surveillance camera was tucked into a corner of the ceiling.

The door from the hallway had a glass panel in it. Probably bullet-proof, she thought. A solid steel door was on the other side of the table. It opened, and a man in an orange jumpsuit, flanked by two uniformed officers, shuffled in. The prisoner had shackles on his ankles and handcuffs on his wrists.

Phyllis caught her breath. The prisoner

was tall and broad-shouldered, and the face under the close-cropped brown hair was instantly familiar to her.

Danny Jackson didn't look exactly like he had the last time she had seen him, too. For one thing, the strain of being tried and convicted of his wife's murder had left his features drawn and haggard.

For another, his face was scraped and bruised, with dried blood and bandages here and there, and his left eye was swollen and sore-looking.

Somebody — or several somebodies — had handed Danny a beating.

CHAPTER 8

Danny recognized Phyllis as well, and he couldn't help but smile despite the pain that must have caused for his battered face. Phyllis wondered if his body was covered with bruises as well.

Before either of them could say anything, D'Angelo shot to his feet and exclaimed, "What the hell! Danny, who did this? This is unacceptable!"

"Take it easy, Mr. D'Angelo," Danny said. "Just a little scuffle at breakfast this morning. It's nothing to worry about."

"Little scuffle?" D'Angelo repeated. "Little scuffle! You've been beaten!"

"Oh, trust me, I did a little damage of my own." Danny sat down in the metal chair opposite the one where Phyllis sat. He looked both happy and relieved. "Mrs. Newsom, I can't tell you how glad I am to see you. It's been a long time."

"I just wish it were under better circumstances," Phyllis said. She wanted to reach across the table and clasp his hands with both of hers, but she figured that wouldn't be allowed and didn't want to do anything that might prompt the guards to cut this interview short.

Still visibly seething, D'Angelo sat down and said, "We can't have you brawling in here, Danny. Not when . . ."

"Not when I've been convicted of beating my wife to death, was that what you were going to say?" Danny's mouth twisted wryly. "Yeah, I guess it would look kind of bad for my appeal if I went around whalin' the tar outta the other prisoners, wouldn't it? I promise you, though, they didn't give me much choice. I had to defend myself."

"Of course you did. I'm going to file a motion to have you moved out of the general population. You shouldn't even be here."

"I know. I'm supposed to be at Huntsville by now, which is even worse, right?"

D'Angelo sighed. "The trouble this morning, was it a spur of the moment thing, or do you have enemies in here who are plotting against you?"

"I just rubbed a couple of the guys wrong from the start, I guess," Danny said with a shrug. "It's not a racial problem or anything like that. Just . . . a lot of the guys in here aren't real friendly characters to start with, you know? It's easy to get on their bad side, and they've always got friends. I don't know how much time they're gonna give us, so let's talk about something else." He smiled at Phyllis again. "It sure was great to see Mike the other day, Mrs. Newsom."

"I know he wishes things were different, too," Phyllis said. "Maybe before too much longer, they will be."

Danny clasped his cuffed hands together in front of him and leaned forward, eagerness on his face as he said, "You've solved the case already, haven't you?"

"I wish I had," Phyllis replied with a slight shake of her head. "Really, though, I've just started looking into it, and so far I haven't found anything we can use to help you."

"I didn't do it, you know."

"I'm sure you —"

"I feel like I need to say that right to your face," Danny went on. "I didn't kill Roxanne. I never would have hurt her. I loved her."

D'Angelo said, "I think we all accept your story, Danny, otherwise we wouldn't be here."

Danny shook his head.

"You don't understand, Mr. D'Angelo. It's really important to me that Mrs. Newsom believe me. You see, she was always kind of like . . . well, kind of like a second mom to me. I spent almost as much time at her house as I did my own. If I thought she believed I was a killer . . . well, I couldn't hardly stand it, that's all."

Evidence or no evidence, Phyllis heard the sincerity and the pain in the young man's voice, and she knew he was telling the truth. She was putting a lot of faith in her own judgment, she was aware of that, but sometimes in life, decisions came down to that. You had to just go with your gut and have faith.

She had faith that Danny Jackson was innocent.

"Don't waste a second worrying about that, Danny," she told him. "I know you didn't do it. Now, let's figure out who did."

A big grin split Danny's face, making him wince as the expression pulled at bruised and scraped flesh.

"What can I do to help you?" he asked.

"Let's start by talking about the salon where Roxanne worked."

"Paul's? What about it?"

"How did Roxanne get along with everyone else there?"

Phyllis could have been mistaken, but she thought a faint, guarded look came into

Danny's eyes as he said, "All right, I guess. It was a place to work and she liked it okay as far as I know. She didn't really complain about it much."

"But she *did* complain about it some?"

"Well, no job is perfect, you know? Especially one where you have to deal with the public. No matter what you do, you're never gonna please everybody, I can tell you that."

Phyllis hadn't considered that angle. She said, "Did Roxanne have trouble with any of the salon's clients?"

"Now and then somebody wouldn't like the way she cut their hair or something. But she didn't talk about it much, just like I didn't talk about the people who didn't like the way Brian and I painted their cars or fixed 'em up. If all you do is complain about your job, that gets old pretty quick. So both of us tried to concentrate on other things when we were together."

"That sounds like a good idea," Phyllis said, nodding. The problem was, that made it more difficult for her to figure out who else might have wanted Roxanne dead. She went on, "I guess she got along all right with Ms. Gibbs."

"Pauline?" Phyllis could see Danny's hesitation and reluctance as he went on, "Pauline's a little like a drill sergeant. Tough as nails. The kind you hammer, not finger-nails."

Somehow, that didn't surprise Phyllis, but she said, "I talked to her and she seemed quite nice."

"Did she think you were a potential client?"

"That's right."

Danny nodded and said, "Yeah, she knows how to sweet-talk customers. She's got that big smile and southern belle accent. My mom used to say about some people, 'Butter wouldn't melt in her mouth.' "

Phyllis nodded. "My mother used to say the same thing. I've probably said it myself."

"Well, that's the way Pauline is around the customers, but once they're gone, she doesn't mind laying into the employees for the least little thing she thinks they've done wrong. The pay is okay, though, so they put up with it. Pauline can afford to pay well, the prices she charges."

Phyllis thought about the appointment she had at the salon. She hoped she wouldn't have to take out a mortgage on the house to keep it.

"Roxanne didn't have any particular trouble with her?"

"No more than any of the other girls, I guess. Not that she told me about, anyway."

"Did she talk about them much? The other girls who work there?"

Danny shook his head, but once again Phyllis got the feeling he wasn't being completely forthcoming. He said, "You went there, right?"

"Yes, but I didn't tell them why I was really there. I pretended to want to have my hair done."

"Did you talk to anybody besides Pauline?"

"A young woman named Aurora," Phyllis said.

This time, a definite flash of alarm was visible in Danny's eyes. He asked, "What did she say? She's kind of a nutjob, you know."

"Really? She seemed nice enough. A little, um, eccentric, maybe."

"What color is her hair this week? The way she keeps changing it, it's gonna all fall out one of these days." Danny laughed, although it didn't sound particularly genuine. "You learn things like that when you're married to a beautician, I guess."

"It was two-tone, actually. Blue and purple. And she had half of it straight while the other half was done up in corn rows."

Danny nodded and said, "Yeah, that's Aurora, all right. She likes to make fun of her grandparents for bein' hippies, but she's kind of a love child herself."

"How did she and Roxanne get along?"

"Fine, I suppose. I don't remember Roxanne ever saying much about her."

"How well did you know her?"

"Aurora? Shoot, not at all. Just to say hello to whenever I stopped by there for some reason."

"How often was that?" Phyllis asked.

"Not often. I might have gone by the salon once or twice a month, sometimes not that often. Sometimes Roxanne forgot and left something at home, and I'd run it by. My shop's on 377, you know, about a mile south of the traffic circle. Not that far from the salon." A wistful look came over Danny's face. "Sometimes I'd go by there and pick her up if she had some time free in the middle of the day, and we'd go eat lunch at one of the Chinese buffets. There's a ton of 'em around there."

Phyllis could tell he was missing those simpler times, and she thought he was sincere about that. Tragedy had ended Roxanne's life and turned his upside-down. He had to know that nothing would ever be the same. Now the best he could hope for was to not spend the next three decades behind bars, but either way, his wife would still be dead.

She wanted to hug him and pat his head, but he wasn't a little boy anymore. She couldn't fix this like putting a band-aid on a cut or mercurochome on a scraped knee. This would require a lot more effort, and it might be painful for everyone involved.

Danny continued, "I tried not to show up at the salon too much, though. I don't think Pauline liked it very much when I did. She didn't want her rich clients seeing a scruffy guy like me coming in and out of the place."

"I'm sure you looked perfectly fine," Phyllis said. "You're a handsome young man, and you weren't wearing . . ."

"You mean I wasn't wearing a jail jumpsuit then." Danny chuckled. "No, but I usually had paint on my clothes. Hard to avoid it in my business."

"I suppose so."

One of the guards opened the door and said, "That's it. Wrap it up."

"I need more time with my client," D'Angelo protested, but Phyllis sensed he was doing it just out of habit, accustomed as he was to wrangling with the authorities.

"You can come back another time, counselor," the officer said.

Danny said, "I hope you come back, too, Mrs. Newsom. It sure was good to see you and talk to you. You'll say hey to Mike for me, won't you?"

"Of course."

Both guards came in and flanked Danny as he got to his feet.

"And thank him for talking to you about my case," he added. "I . . . I'm really counting on you." He nodded to D'Angelo. "On both of you."

The guards led him out. D'Angelo folded back the sheets on the legal pad he had filled with notes while Phyllis and Danny were talking. They didn't say anything to each other as they followed the corridors back to the lobby where Sam was waiting.

As they stepped into the lobby, though, where there was a constant buzz of conversation and no one could eavesdrop on them easily, D'Angelo paused and said quietly, "A time or two there, I thought I saw a strange look on that boy's face."

"I know," Phyllis said. "I saw the same thing. He's lying about something. We're going to have to figure out what."

CHAPTER 9

Sam stood up as they came toward him. He asked, "Find out anything?", then before either of them could answer, he went on, "I reckon it'd probably be better to talk about it somewhere else, though, wouldn't it?"

"That's right," D'Angelo said. He turned to Phyllis and added, "Let's get together at my office this afternoon. Say, two o'clock?"

"We'll be there," Phyllis said. "That will give me time to talk things over with Sam." He was the most important sounding board she had.

They left the jail, going different directions when they reached the sidewalk. Phyllis and Sam went back to the pickup. Sam drove down along the river as he headed toward the Interstate.

Phyllis wasn't able to reproduce the interview verbatim, but she came pretty close. Sam listened in attentive silence until she was finished, then said, "I didn't see that

Aurora girl myself, but you say she was pretty good-lookin'?"

"Very attractive, as long as you don't mind all the, well, odd things that young women do to themselves these days."

"And Danny sorta looked uneasy when you brought her up?"

"He did. He also said he barely knew her. Do you think that means anything?"

Sam shrugged. "When a young fella claims he hasn't been payin' any attention to a girl, it's usually a sign that he's noticed her, all right. Maybe more than just noticed."

"He's eight or ten years older than her," Phyllis pointed out. "Although I suppose that's not really a huge age difference, is it?"

"Not enough to rule out something goin' on between 'em."

"But that's just pure speculation, Sam, based on nothing more than a very brief reaction on Danny's part."

"Sure. But it might explain why Aurora sulled up a little when you mentioned Roxanne. If she had her sights set on Danny, that'd make Roxanne the competition."

Phyllis frowned in thought as she looked out the window. They were on the freeway now, heading back through Arlington

Heights toward the western part of Fort Worth, but Phyllis didn't really see the heavily populated landscape passing by. She was thinking about the way Aurora had reacted when she asked about Roxanne, and Phyllis had to admit that Sam had a point. It could have been good old-fashioned jealousy because Aurora had feelings for Danny herself.

Had Danny returned those feelings, or was he just embarrassed because Aurora had a crush on him . . . if indeed she did?

"I want to see some of the other places," Phyllis said.

"The other places involved in the case, you mean?"

"That's right. Danny's shop, and the house where they lived."

"The murder didn't take place at either of those."

"I know," Phyllis said. "I just want to get a little better feel for the people involved."

Sam nodded and said, "Makes sense, I guess. You know where to find them?"

"Mr. D'Angelo won't be back in his office yet, but I should be able to get the addresses from his secretary," Phyllis said as she took out her phone. "Danny mentioned that his shop is on Highway 377, south of the traffic circle, so I guess you can head in that general direction while I'm doing that."

"Will do," Sam said.

He exited from the freeway just past Ridgmar Mall and took the looping ramp that put him onto U.S. Highway 183, headed southbound. A couple of miles ahead was the Weatherford Traffic Circle, a relic of the 1950s, where U.S. 377 split off and headed south-by-southwest toward Granbury. There were several red lights along the way to slow them down, and by the time they reached the circle, Phyllis had the addresses they needed.

As Sam watched the traffic and navigated the sometimes confusing circle, he said, "You know, in England they call these roundabouts. This one's not too bad, but I always hated the one in Waco. Took the wrong turn off of it more times than I like to think about. Then I always had to wander around until I could find my way back and try again."

"I thought you had a GPS in your head," Phyllis said with a smile.

"Naw, not back then. GPS hadn't been invented yet."

That made her laugh out loud. Then she started watching the street numbers. A moment later she pointed and said, "There."

The building that housed Lone Star Paint

and Body had started out as white stucco, but time, weather, and exhaust fumes from the heavily traveled highway had turned it a dirty gray. It looked like a typical garage with two big doors opening into the bays where work was done, with a smaller door leading into an office to the left. The business sat on a good-sized lot, the rear portion of which was enclosed by a high chain link fence with a locked gate in it. That area was paved with gravel. Several cars were parked back there, probably vehicles that hadn't been picked up yet by their owners. Maybe the paint jobs on them were still drying, Phyllis thought.

There were three parking spaces in front of the office, all of them empty at the moment. Sam pulled the pickup into one of them. He and Phyllis got out and walked toward the nearest bay. The rolling doors at the front of both bays were lifted. A white crossover was in the farthest one. In the closer one was a shiny black pickup with a raised suspension and oversized tires. The smell of paint was strong in the air, along with a few other chemicals. It was almost overpowering.

Someone was banging on something on the other side of the pickup. Phyllis and Sam walked around the back of it and found

101

a man in white coveralls down on one knee by the front fender, his body twisted around so he could reach up inside the wheel well and hit something with a rubber mallet.

He saw them and stopped what he was doing, untwisting from the awkward position and standing up. As he set the mallet on the black pickup's hood, he smiled and said, "Hi, folks. If you need to see about getting some work done, we'll have to go in the office. Customers aren't really supposed to be out here. Insurance regulations, you know."

He was tall and broad-shouldered, with tousled blond hair and a handsome face. Phyllis couldn't tell if his beard stubble was fashionable or if he just hadn't bothered to shave for a few days. She thought he looked like a California surfer, or at least what the movies made California surfers look like.

"What if we *didn't* stop in to see about hiring you?" Phyllis asked.

The man nodded toward an inside door that led into the office and said, "We still need to go inside. But what brings you here if you don't have a car that needs worked on?"

"Your partner, Danny Jackson," Phyllis said. "You *are* Brian Flynn, aren't you?" She didn't see anyone else working, and from what she had heard about the shop, it was a low-budget operation, run by just the two partners.

The man frowned. "Lady, you don't look like a reporter, and you sure don't look like a cop. Neither does your friend. So I don't have anything to say to you."

"We're trying to help Danny." Phyllis had decided to put their cards on the table. "We just came from talking to him at the jail. We're working with the lawyer handling Danny's appeal."

"The two of you?" The man clearly had a hard time believing that. "What are you, private eyes?" The look on his face said that was a ridiculous idea.

"Sort of," Sam said. His voice was harder and flatter than Phyllis had ever heard it. "We're investigators, and like my partner just told you, we're workin' for Danny's lawyer. I hear tell you're his friend. If that's true, you'll want to talk to us . . . because we may be his only way out of a one-way ticket to Huntsville."

The man looked surprised and a little embarrassed. He said, "Hey, I didn't mean any offense. It's just that —"

"We're not exactly young," Sam said. "We know that. Our brains work just as well as they ever did, though, and that's what Danny's dependin' on."

"I'm sorry. Of course you're right. Let's go inside. I'm Brian Flynn, by the way. You were right about that, ma'am."

"I'm Phyllis Newsom," Phyllis introduced herself as they walked toward the door. "This is Sam Fletcher."

"I'm pleased to meet you. I —" Brian Flynn stopped short and turned his head to look at them. "Wait a minute. I remember Danny talking about a woman who lives over in Weatherford, the mother of his best friend from school. He said he used to hang around at her house a lot when he was a kid, and that now she solves murders, of all things!"

"That'd be Phyllis," Sam said, leaning his head toward her.

"Then it really is an honor to meet you. Maybe you really can help Danny."

"We're going to do our best," Phyllis said.

A window unit hummed in one of the office's two windows, pumping out cool air. Even better than the temperature was the fact that the paint smell wasn't nearly as strong inside the office, although it didn't go away completely. It was a lot more bearable, though.

There were two desks, both on the small side, each with a computer and monitor, along with a couple of filing cabinets, a free-standing set of metal shelves with various auto body parts on them, and a short sofa upholstered with fake leather that had seen better days. It was peeling and threadbare in several places. A short refrigerator was tucked into a corner. A calendar hanging on the wall above the refrigerator had a picture of some sort of racing car on it. Phyllis wasn't sure, but she thought the car was the kind that people used to call a dragster. She had no idea what they were called these days.

Brian Flynn said, "Have a seat," and since the only place to sit down other than plastic chairs behind the desks was the sofa, Phyllis and Sam settled down on it. "Can I get you something to drink? There are Cokes and Dr Peppers and bottled water in the fridge."

Phyllis shook her head, and Sam said, "Nope, I reckon we're good. Thanks, though."

Brian went behind one of the desks and sat down. "You said you just talked to Danny?"

"That's right," Phyllis said.

Brian leaned forward and asked, "How's he doing?" Then, quickly, before Phyllis or Sam could answer, he shook his head and went on, "No, that's a stupid question. He's in jail, and he's going to prison for murdering his wife. He can't be doing any good."

"Actually, it's worse than that," Phyllis said. "He got in a fight with some of the other prisoners this morning, so he's kind of beaten up right now."

Brian's hands clenched into fists on the desk in front of him. He looked like he wanted to curse, but he held it in. He sat back, shook his head, and muttered, "It's not right. It's just not right."

"You don't think he did it?"

Brian reached over to the other desk and picked up a framed photograph that was sitting where Phyllis and Sam couldn't see it. He turned the picture around and set it on his desk facing them.

"Does that look like a guy who could ever hurt his wife?"

The couple in the photo were at a lake somewhere, standing together on the beach and smiling into the camera while sailboats with bright sails cut across the water behind them. Phyllis recognized Danny right away. He wore swimming trunks and a t-shirt. The woman beside him with light brown hair was in cut-off jeans and a bikini top. She was considerably shorter than him. She had her left arm around his waist, and his right arm was looped around her shoulders. They looked young, healthy, happy, and totally at ease with each other.

"Just look at 'em," Brian went on. "You can tell they're, like, completely in love with each other."

That was the way it looked to Phyllis, and when she glanced over at Sam, he shrugged and nodded, indicating that he agreed with Brian, too.

"That was taken last summer, Fourth of July, up on Eagle Mountain Lake. Less than a year later the cops were saying he killed Roxanne. I didn't believe it then, and I don't believe it now." Brian blew out an exasperated-sounding breath. "I just wish I'd been here that evening so I could've given Danny an alibi. He left here at eight forty-five, got to the salon and found Roxie and called 911 a couple of minutes before nine. He wouldn't have had time to hurt her like that."

"How do you know he left at eight forty-five?" Phyllis asked.

Brian frowned and said, "Well . . . that's what he told me when I talked to him later. I don't have any reason not to believe him. I just couldn't testify to it in court and prove he was telling the truth."

Sam asked, "Was it unusual for one of you to stay late workin' like that?"

Brian shook his head, saying, "No, not really. We took all the jobs we could get. With money so tight, you've sort of got to. Sometimes we got backed up and had to work late to get the cars finished by the time we promised them to the owners. If it takes longer than what they're expecting, they don't come back next time they need some work done."

"You both worked late?" Phyllis said.

"Sometimes me, sometimes Danny, sometimes both of us," Brian said. A frown creased his forehead. "All these questions are starting to seem a little funny. You're supposed to be helping Danny by finding out who really killed his wife, right?"

"That's the idea," Phyllis admitted.

"That doesn't have anything to do with the shop," Brian said, spreading his hands. "She was killed at the salon. She hardly ever came down here. I don't blame her. It's kind of dirty and noisy and smelly around here, and that's on a good day."

"We're looking at everything in Roxanne's life, and in Danny's, too," Phyllis said. "Right now we really don't know enough to suspect anything or anybody."

"Well . . . I guess that makes sense. For a minute there, I just got worried that you thought *I* might've had something to do with her death."

"Not at all," Phyllis said — not because she believed Brian Flynn to be innocent, but because it was just too soon to know, like she had told him.

"You married, Brian?" Sam asked.

"No. I figure I'll settle down one of these days . . . but that day's not here yet."

"How'd you and Danny wind up puttin' in this shop together?"

"We knew each other over in the sand-box."

"Sandbox?" Phyllis repeated.

"Iraq," Sam and Brian said at the same time.

"Oh. You were in the army together."

"That's right." Brian smiled. "Grew up twenty miles apart, him over in Weatherford and me here in Benbrook, and they had to send us to the other side of the world for us to meet."

"From what my son said, I didn't think Danny saw any combat."

"He didn't. Neither of us did. We rotated in and out of the place during one of the relatively peaceful stretches and spent all of our time working on vehicles. We used to hear mortar attacks and small arms fire and IEDs going off, but none of it ever came close to us."

"You were lucky," Sam said.

Brian nodded and said, "Don't I know it. Anyway, after we got to be friends over there, we talked about going into business together when we got home. It seemed like a good idea, and this is the sort of work we knew, so . . ." He shrugged. "We've been at it for a few years now."

"Has it been successful?" Phyllis asked. She already had a pretty good idea what the answer was, but she wanted to know what Brian would say.

"We've kept our heads above water," he replied. "Just barely sometimes. It takes a while to build a business."

"You made it past the first year," Sam pointed out. "Most of 'em don't, statistically speakin'."

"Yeah, but now it's just me. I don't know if I can do enough work to keep the place afloat, and anybody I could hire for what I can afford to pay wouldn't be any good." Brian shook his head. "Right now I'm just doing the best I can and taking it one day at a time. It's a cliché, I know, but what else can I do?"

"Well, we wish you luck," Phyllis said.

"There's something else you can do," Brian said. "Find out who killed Roxanne

110

and get Danny out of jail, so he can come back here and give a guy a hand!"

CHAPTER 10

"Well, if you went in there thinkin' that fella was a suspect," Sam said as they drove away from the paint and body shop a few minutes later, "I reckon it didn't pan out very well."

"You don't think there's any chance he could have killed Roxanne?" Phyllis asked.

"Why would he? As far as I can see, Danny bein' in jail hasn't done anything except put him in a bind. He's liable to lose his business. He doesn't have any motive for hurting Danny *or* Roxanne."

"What if it was a crime of passion?"

Sam glanced over at her but didn't take his eyes off the road for long.

"You mean if there was somethin' goin' on between Brian and Roxanne?"

"He's a good-looking young man, she was a good-looking young woman —"

"A good-looking young married woman."

"If the past few years have taught us anything, Sam, it's that a lot of people don't take their marriage vows very seriously."

"I always did," he said.

"So did I. But we've seen plenty of evidence to the contrary."

"That's true, I suppose," he admitted. "Depressin'ly so, sometimes."

"Yes." Phyllis nodded slowly. "But we have absolutely nothing to indicate that might be the case here. I suppose I could ask Danny about it . . ."

"He might not give you a straight answer," Sam cautioned. "They might've kept it a secret from him, or he might not want to admit it, even to himself." He frowned in thought. "I suppose I could drop in on some of the other businesses around there and maybe ask if anybody ever saw Roxanne over there when Danny wasn't around. Once or twice might be a coincidence, but more than that . . ."

That wasn't a bad idea, Phyllis thought. Sam might not be a veteran detective, but with his aw-shucks, friendly-old-geezer demeanor, he could get anybody talking about almost anything without them ever realizing he was pumping them for information.

"That's worth a try," she said. "In the meantime, let's go take a look at the house."

In a few minutes they were on Loop 820,

heading north. Sam took the exit for Silver Creek Road and followed it on its winding path through the country. The tall buildings of downtown Fort Worth were visible in the distance, back to the east. Also in that direction but closer was the Lockheed-Martin aircraft plant.

In the other direction, though, lay rolling hills dotted with clumps of trees. Some of them had large, round bales of hay harvested earlier in the summer scattered across them. Horses and cows grazed here and there, and the pickup went past a couple of sheds built to give the animals shelter. Sam drove by a fenced-in area where a couple of natural gas storage tanks were located. Houses, most of them at the far end of long driveways, were few and far between.

It was a striking contrast. Turn your head one way and you saw a bustling metropolis. Look the other way and a peaceful, rural landscape was laid out before your eyes. That wasn't really uncommon in Texas, though. Phyllis supposed it was that way in other places, too.

"I think that may be the mailbox coming up on the left," she said to Sam. "You'd better slow down."

Sam took his foot off the gas. When they

got close enough for Phyllis to read the number painted on the side of the mailbox, she went on, "That's it, all right."

"No police tape blockin' the gate," Sam commented. "Of course, the murder didn't happen here, and once the cops searched the house to make sure there was no evidence layin' around, they would've been done with it."

The opening in the fence that ran along the front edge of the property didn't have an actual gate in it, only a cattle guard across the road. Sam turned in, bumped across that barrier made of pipes set horizontally into the ground, and started up the dirt and gravel driveway.

"How big is this property?" he asked. "I wouldn't have thought they could afford much acreage."

"We can probably find out," Phyllis said. "From the looks of the surrounding countryside, this was a big ranch at one time. Whoever owns it may have sold just the house and the area around it and kept the rest of the acreage intact. Say, if the original owner passed away while living here, and the heirs didn't want to keep the house but did want the rest of the property. If that's the case, it's probably only three or four acres."

"Which still wouldn't be cheap," Sam pointed out.

"Remember, it was established at the trial that Danny and Roxanne had sunk all their savings into the place and gone into debt to buy it and fix it up. Those money problems are supposed to be what caused the arguments between them."

Sam nodded as he brought the pickup to a stop in front of the ranch house. He said, "Yeah, that all makes sense."

The house was obviously old but had been well taken care of, Phyllis thought as she studied the white-painted frame structure with dark green trim and shingles. A front porch with flower beds in front of it ran the width of the building. There were flowers in those beds, but weeds had popped up as well, because there was no one here to pull them. The St. Augustine in the small yard was unmowed and even taller Johnson grass had encroached on it in places.

Sam frowned and said, "I hate Johnson grass. Reckon it'd be all right if I got out and pulled some o' that?"

"I don't see why anyone would care," Phyllis told him.

Both of them got out of the pickup. Sam started pulling up the Johnson grass by the roots and tossing it aside while Phyllis

116

walked slowly to one side of the house. It had gotten a fresh coat of paint within the past couple of years, she estimated. The screens on the numerous windows were all in good repair. Two rocking chairs sat on the porch, and she could imagine Danny and Roxanne sitting out there on a pleasant evening.

"I wonder what's going to happen to the place," she said.

"You mean if Danny doesn't come back to live here?" Sam said. "More than likely the bank will take it over. You said they borrowed money to buy it and fix it up, right?"

"That's right," Phyllis said. "Danny can't very well pay off that debt if he's in prison."

Still bent over pulling weeds, Sam went on, "And if the bank doesn't get it, the county will for unpaid taxes. They'll auction it off, and somebody'll get a good deal."

"Not if we can prove that Danny's innocent, though. Even if he doesn't want to live here anymore — and I can understand why he wouldn't — he could at least sell the place and have some money to make a new start."

"That's what we'll hope for." Sam straightened, putting his hands in the small of his back to help himself get aligned. He nodded toward the road and said, "Somebody's comin'."

The vehicle coming up the driveway toward them was also a pickup, but it was older and more beat-up than Sam's. The driver didn't appear to be in any hurry. When the truck came to a stop, the door swung open and a gray-haired woman stepped out. She wore boots, jeans, and an unbuttoned, long-sleeved flannel shirt over a t-shirt. The pickup had a gun rack in its rear window that held a pump shotgun and what Phyllis thought of as a deer rifle, although she was no expert on firearms.

The woman didn't smile, but she seemed friendly enough as she said, "Hello. Is this place gonna be for sale?"

"I don't have any idea," Phyllis said.

"I was in the field over there across the road —" The woman jerked her head in that direction. "— feedin' my horses, when I saw you folks pull in here. Thought you might be real estate people. The young fella who owns the property is in jail, and I figured he might need to sell it to help pay his legal bills."

"In jail?" Phyllis said, deciding on the spur of the moment not to reveal who she and Sam were and what they were doing here.

"Yeah. He killed his wife."

Phyllis let her eyes get wide. "How terrible!" She cast a nervous glance toward the house. "Did it happen . . . here?"

"Oh, no," the woman said with a shake of her head. "It was over in town somewhere, at the beauty shop where the wife worked. You might've seen somethin' about it in the paper a while back, but I suppose you wouldn't have any reason to remember it, or connect it up with this property, even if you did."

"I like to paint scenes of old farmhouses and ranch houses," Phyllis said, still improvising. Sam, bless his heart, stood by looking like he was in total agreement with everything she said. She went on, "I thought maybe I'd ask the owner if I could take a picture of it, so I could do some sketches later on and maybe turn it into a painting. It sounds like there's no one here, though."

"Nope, the place is pretty much abandoned now." The woman waved a hand at the house. "You can go ahead and take as many pictures of it as you want, though. As far as I know, nobody would care."

With the woman having said that, Phyllis figured she had better keep up the fiction. She took her phone from her pocket, opened the camera function, and started taking pictures of the house from various angles. Actually, that wasn't a bad idea, she told herself. Given everything she had learned so far about the case, she didn't expect the house to turn out to be important, but you never knew. It didn't hurt to have as much information as you could gather.

To that end, she said to the gray-haired woman, "You keep horses in the field across the road?"

"Yeah. The acreage has been in my family for close to eighty years. I live a couple of miles away in White Settlement. Name's Estelle Prentice."

"Pleased to meet you, Miz Prentice," Sam said. "I'm Sam, and this is Phyllis."

The woman didn't press him for last names. She said, "It's Mrs. Prentice. I'm a widow."

"Sorry. I was sayin' M-I-Z, though, sort of slurrin' the Missus, instead of M-S."

Estelle Prentice laughed and said, "I should have known. You're an old-timer like me and don't have enough time left to be politically correct."

Sam just shrugged. Phyllis knew the last thing he wanted to do was get involved in a political discussion of any sort.

"How many horses do you have?" he asked.

"Four. Don't really need 'em at my age, but I'm used to having them, I guess."

"Did you know the couple who lived here?" Phyllis asked.

"Danny and Roxanne? A little. My shed's by the road, and they stopped once when I was out there and introduced themselves to me. Roxanne, she liked horses. Said that one of these days she might get one. They have enough acreage here around the house to support one."

"They just own the land around the house?"

"Yeah. All the land on this side of the road for a mile or more used to be the old Chamberlain ranch. Ben Chamberlain settled here in the 1880s and built that old stone house you can see over there." Estelle pointed to a hilltop about half a mile away to the south. "From what I've heard, it used to be the first stagecoach stop west of Fort Worth. They'd switch teams every eight to ten miles."

"That's fascinating," Phyllis murmured.

Sam said, "Does the Chamberlain family still own the rest of the land hereabouts?"

"Some of it," Estelle replied. "If you came from the direction of town, you passed a little side road to get here. That side road leads up over the hill and on the other side the family's been breaking up the acreage and selling it to housing developers." She frowned. "You can't see 'em from here, but they've started building and in a few years there'll be hundreds of houses not half a mile away. Reckon it's only a matter of time until the family breaks up the whole place."

"Why'd they sell off this house, then?" Sam asked, nodding toward it.

"That's the first thing they sold. The ranch foreman used to live here, back in the old days. I think they planned to break up this side of the property first and develop it themselves, but then there was some talk about how it was easier to connect up with the utilities on the other side of the hill . . ." Estelle shook her head. "I don't know the details. But they changed the plan and started in from the other direction. It's inevitable, though. Whichever way they go about it, sooner or later this'll all be covered with those damn brick houses that all look alike, crammed together like a rat's nest."

Sam nodded in solemn agreement.

"They won't get my land, though," Estelle went on. "My kids'll probably sell it when I'm gone, along with my horses and everything else, but I'll be too dead to care then."

"I guess we can't expect our children to always think the same things are important that we do," Phyllis said.

"Not this day and age, that's for damn sure."

"The people who bought this house, were they an older couple?"

"Danny and Roxanne?" Estelle shook her head. "No, they were just kids. Early thirties, maybe? We never really talked enough for me to know for sure. They were a little different, though, Roxanne especially. Seemed like a really nice girl. She said she'd always wanted a place like this in the country. And like I told you, she wanted to get a horse sometime. Danny, well, he went along with her, of course, but I don't think he really cared that much either way. He just wanted to do whatever would make her happy. I sure was surprised when he killed her. Didn't see that comin' at all."

Phyllis put her phone away and said, "I suppose we've taken up enough of your time, Estelle . . ."

"Oh, shoot, I'm glad to talk. You could probably tell that about me. My late husband, he was one of those fellas you had to pry the words out of with a crowbar. Funny thing is, other folks would tell me that he talked all the time around them."

"Sometimes it just works out that way," Sam said.

Estelle said goodbye, got back in her

truck, backed around, and drove off, raising a cloud of dust from the driveway. Phyllis and Sam waited until it blew away, then followed suit.

"Head for home now?" Sam asked as he pulled out onto the loop.

"Yes, although if you want to stop somewhere for lunch along the way, that would be fine with me. It's getting pretty late."

"Sounds good to me. What did you think of the place?"

"It looks like Roxanne and Danny were turning it into a real home," Phyllis said. "From what Mrs. Prentice said, Roxanne was really the one who wanted to buy the house and fix it up."

"Yeah. You know what was gonna happen, though, when all those new houses came flowin' over the hill like a tide."

"The property was going to get more valuable. They would have been able to sell it to a developer, get out of debt, and make some profit on top of that."

"That's my guess," Sam said. "Danny might've wanted to sell. The money from a deal like that could've gone a long way toward keepin' the paint and body shop afloat. But if Roxanne didn't want to sell, a disagreement like that could lead to a bad argument."

"The same thought went through my head. And then something else occurred to me?"

"What's that?"

"What we've found is a pretty good motive for Danny to commit murder," Phyllis said, "and that's just the opposite of what we're trying to do!"

"But facts are facts."

"Yes," she said. "Unfortunately, they are."

CHAPTER 11

They stopped at a steakhouse in Willow Park for lunch, then drove on to Weatherford. When they were on the outskirts of town, Phyllis's cell phone rang. She took it out of her pocket, looked at the display, and saw an unfamiliar number.

"Probably just one of those recorded junk calls," she said.

"I like the one that starts out 'Hello, seniors!' " Sam said. "That fella always sounds so dang cheerful."

"I suppose I'd better answer it." Phyllis swiped the screen with her finger, held the phone to her ear, and said, "Hello?"

A woman's voice said, "Mrs. Newsom?"

"That's right."

"This is Aurora at Paul's Beauty Salon. I'm calling to let you know we've had a cancellation, and we can see you at ten-thirty tomorrow morning if you'd like to come in."

"So soon? I was just there yesterday."

"That's the way these things work out sometimes," Aurora said.

"Well, then, of course, that's fine." Phyllis wasn't going to pass up a chance to find out more about the place where Roxanne Jackson had worked. "I appreciate you letting me know."

"I've got you down for ten-thirty, then. We'll see you in the morning."

"Thanks," Phyllis said, then broke the connection.

"Goin' on a cruise, buyin' a security system, or lowerin' the interest rate on your credit cards?" Sam asked with a smile.

"I have a ten-thirty appointment tomorrow morning at Paul's Beauty Salon."

"I sort of figured as much, from the way you were talkin'. I was just jokin' about those other things." Sam grew more serious. "Got you in in a hurry, didn't they? I thought it was supposed to be a couple of weeks."

"According to Aurora, they had a cancellation. It's strange. I didn't actually see the cancellation list on her computer, but I got the impression it was long enough I wouldn't have been anywhere near the top. I mean, it wouldn't be surprising if they called a few other people first and they

127

couldn't come in tomorrow, but . . ."

"But this is almost like they moved you all the way to the top on purpose."

Phyllis nodded and said, "That's the way it seems to me."

"You can't prove it, though."

"Not at all. And why would they do something like that? It's suspicious."

"Maybe somebody there is suspicious of *you.*"

"Because I came in asking questions and brought up Roxanne?" Phyllis nodded again, slowly, as she frowned in thought. "I suppose that's possible. But only if the someone you're talking about has something to hide. It could only be Aurora or Pauline. I didn't talk to anyone else."

"So you're gonna keep the appointment?"

"Of course."

"Maybe I better come with you," Sam said. "There was a good place to sit, you said, and I could take a book with me. Fellas must wait there for their ladies from time to time."

Phyllis smiled and said, "Am I your lady, Sam?"

"Reckon you would've known that by now."

"I do," Phyllis said, then went on, "But I don't think anything's going to happen to

128

me in a beauty salon with a lot of other people around."

"Not likely, but you never know. I sure don't mind taggin' along. Anyway, it gives me an excuse to sit and read for a while."

"You're retired. You can sit and read any time you want to."

"Yeah, but after leadin' such a busy life for so long, sometimes it's hard to slow down. I feel guilty when I'm not up doin' something."

"I know the feeling," Phyllis said. "Of course, you can come along. I'm always happy to have your company. Also, it'll give you a chance to talk to Aurora. Maybe you'll find out more than I could. She might see you as the kindly old grandfather type. Only her grandfather was a hippy."

Sam grinned, held up his right hand with the first two fingers spread in a peace sign and said, "Far out, dude."

When they got back to the house, they found Carolyn in the kitchen with several mixing bowls spread out on the counter and a perplexed look on her face.

"I'm doing something wrong," she said, "but I can't figure out what."

"I'd be glad to help," Phyllis said as she started toward the counter and tried to see what was in the bowls.

Carolyn moved to block her view. "No, that's all right," she said quickly. "This is for that recipe I'm going to enter in the magazine contest, and even though we decided that it would be all right for me to send it in, I think it'll still look better if there's no input from you, Phyllis. No offense."

"None taken," Phyllis said, although in truth she was a little surprised by Carolyn's attitude. It was her right to do as she saw fit, though. "Do I get to sample the result when you're done?"

"I don't know." Carolyn frowned. "Sam's here. He's always a good taste tester."

"This is for a pie contest, right?" Sam asked. "I'm your huckleberry!"

Both women looked at him. Carolyn said, "What?"

"It's a line from a movie. *Tombstone.* When Doc Holliday's gettin' ready to have a gunfight with somebody . . . Well, never mind. I'll be happy to sample anything you come up with, Carolyn, that's all I'm sayin'."

"It's not huckleberry pie," Carolyn said. "Although . . ." She shook her head. "No, never mind."

"Berry," Phyllis said, also looking as if

thoughts had started to race through her head.

Sam held up his hands, palms out, and said as he angled toward the hall, "I'm gonna leave you ladies to it, whatever it is."

He went on toward the living room. Knowing that Carolyn didn't want to talk about her recipe or the magazine contest, Phyllis changed the subject by saying, "The girl at the beauty salon where Roxanne worked called a little while ago. They had a cancellation, and I'm going in to get my hair done tomorrow morning."

"That soon?"

"Sam and I thought it seemed a little fishy, too," Phyllis said. "But on the other hand, it's a good chance to try to find out more."

Carolyn cocked her head to the side and said, "There's nothing wrong with your hair the way it is now. What are you going to have them do?"

"I don't know." Phyllis's hair was mostly gray but retained some of its natural brown color. She wore it in a fairly short and simple style that was easy to take care of. But maybe one of the stylists at Paul's could do something with it, she thought. It didn't hurt anything to have a new look every once in a while.

Phyllis heard the front door open and

close and wondered if Sam was going somewhere. But then she heard a familiar voice call, "I'm back!" and knew someone had come in, not gone out.

"That's Eve," Carolyn said with a look of pleased surprise on her face. "I didn't think she was supposed to be back until tomorrow."

"You know how those show business types are," Phyllis said with a smile as she and Carolyn started toward the living room. "Unpredictable!"

When they came into the room, Sam was hugging Eve Turner. She turned to Phyllis and Carolyn and swept toward them like a force of nature. They welcomed her home with a group hug, including even the usually reserved Carolyn.

"Did you meet a bunch of movie stars?" Sam asked.

"Not really," Eve said. "But I did see Channing Tatum in the same restaurant where I was eating one night."

"I don't know who that is," Carolyn said.

"An absolutely gorgeous young man, dear. He was in those movies about the male dancers — Never mind, you wouldn't have seen those." Eve smiled. "But I own the Blu-Rays, if you'd like to watch them sometime."

"Where are your bags?" Phyllis asked.

"The taxi driver put them on the porch. I'd better get them —"

"I'll handle that," Sam said. "You ladies just go on with your visitin'. I know you've got a lot to catch up on."

"I want to hear all about Hollywood," Phyllis said. She wasn't obsessed with celebrities like so many people seemed to be, but she did think the entertainment business was interesting, in a way.

Carolyn said, "And Phyllis can tell you about the murder she's trying to solve."

Eve's eyes opened wider as she looked at Phyllis. "Another murder? Really? That's perfect!"

"Well . . . not for the victim."

"No, no, of course not, but it'll keep interest in the property up."

"The property?"

"My book. The intellectual property."

"Of course," Phyllis said, nodding.

"Are they still making a movie out of it?" Carolyn asked as Sam carried in a couple of Eve's bags and started up the stairs with them.

Eve sank down on the sofa and sighed. "The producer who took the option on it wasn't able to get it greenlit at the studio he's associated with. It's stuck in development hell."

Carolyn slowly shook her head and said, "I don't know what that means."

"But he's talking about trying to sell it to one of the cable channels as a TV series," Eve said, brightening.

"Like HBO?"

"Not HBO." Eve waved a hand in dismissal of that idea. "It doesn't skew gritty enough. There's not enough sex and violence."

"Well, I should hope not," Phyllis said. "We're retired teachers."

"Yes, dear, but you keep getting involved in all those murders, and some of us . . . Well, never mind. Let's just say that right now, we're not sure what's going to happen. Something *will* happen, though, sooner or later. I'm sure of it. In the meantime, the book comes out this winter, and once it takes off, that will jump-start those people in Hollywood."

"I hope so," Phyllis said. She knew how excited Eve was about everything that was going on, and she didn't want to see her old friend disappointed.

"In the meantime, tell me about this murder you're mixed up in," Eve said, leaning forward. "Wait, *don't* tell me. You've figured out who the killer is, right?"

"Not yet," Phyllis said. "There are a lot of

strands to this case, but so far none of them have led anywhere."

"They will. I have complete faith in you. You saved *me* from a murder charge, remember?"

"I'm not likely to forget any time soon. In this case, though, the person charged with the murder has already been convicted. He's behind bars."

"Well, you have to get him out! Justice must be served!"

Justice, Phyllis thought. And Hollywood.

CHAPTER 12

Having Eve back home made everything seem better, Phyllis thought. The place hadn't exactly been empty without her, but the four of them were sort of like the Four Musketeers, as Sam had been known to claim.

"And I'm D'Artagnan," he would always add.

"I wouldn't know how to use a sword or a musket," Carolyn had said the last time he brought it up. "I'm just glad you didn't call us the Four Stooges." She shuddered a little at the thought.

"There were actually six Stooges in all . . . seven if you count Ted Healy, who started the act —"

That was as far as the conversation had gotten before it moved on, thankfully, to something else.

During the afternoon, at supper, and then during the evening, most of the discussion centered around Eve's trip to Hollywood. She had plenty of stories to tell about the fancy hotel where she had stayed, the restaurants where she had eaten, the producers she had met, and the movie stars she had seen, which turned out to be more than just Channing Tatum.

Eve was happy to monopolize the conversation, but she stopped now and then to ask about things that had happened in Weatherford while she was gone, and eventually, that brought out in bits and pieces the story of Phyllis and Sam's investigation into Roxanne Jackson's murder.

"I'm surprised you haven't solved it yet, dear," Eve said as they all sat in the living room. "You've been looking into it for, what, two days now?"

"It takes time to figure things out," Phyllis said, then added dryly, "And who knows, one of these days I might *not* solve it."

Eve shook her head and declared, "Oh, no, I don't believe that. Failure is not an option, as the old saying goes."

"Because it would be bad for sales of your book."

"Because it would be bad for that unjustly accused and convicted young man. If he really didn't kill his wife, he shouldn't be locked up for it. That just wouldn't be fair."

Sam put in, "There's another old sayin' about life not bein' fair."

"Yes, but it *should* be, whenever that's possible," Eve said. "And if we don't strive for that, then what's the point?"

Flighty and shallow she might be, Phyllis thought — or at least might *appear* to be — but Eve still had the knack of putting her finger on the core of things. Phyllis supposed that was what made her a good writer.

She was in her bedroom later, with her laptop open on the desk, when Sam knocked softly on the door and came in.

"Goin' back over the stuff in the newspapers about the case?" he asked her as he looked over her shoulder at the screen.

"Yes, just to make sure I don't forget anything I want to try to work into the conversation at the salon tomorrow morning. I may not get another chance to talk to the people who work there. It would look funny, after all, if I kept coming back."

"You could always claim they didn't make you beautiful enough. Of course, I don't know who'd ever believe that."

Without looking around, she swatted him lightly on the hip and said, "That'll be enough flattery, Sam Fletcher. We're both far too old for that."

"One more old sayin' . . . you're only as

old as you feel." He bent over and kissed the top of her head. "And you make me feel like a young fella of sixty. But I'll leave you to your studyin'. It's important."

"I know," Phyllis said. "I'm not sure if it's because Danny's going to be transferred to Huntsville any day now or if it's something else, but I keep having the feeling that time is running out."

Sam took an old paperback Western novel with him the next morning, but he had his phone, too, if he wanted to read something on it. Phyllis wasn't exactly nervous as they drove toward Fort Worth in Sam's pickup. She had taken part in enough investigations by now that this was nothing new.

But at the same time, you never knew what was going to happen when you started poking around in people's lives. There was always a chance things would take you by surprise, and in dealing with murder, that could be dangerous. It was easy enough to say that nothing too bad was going to happen in a beauty salon . . .

But it had to Roxanne Jackson, hadn't it?

Sam must have sensed that something was bothering her, because he said, "I'll be right there, you know, where I can keep an eye on you the whole time."

"Oh, I know that," Phyllis said. "I'm not really afraid. There's just so much riding on this for Danny."

"Years of his life," Sam agreed. "Decades, more than likely. Not to mention his own good name. I can't imagine what it'd be like to have folks believe that you murdered somebody you love, when you didn't do it."

"It must be sheer torture for him. Maybe it won't be too long before we can help him."

"We're tryin', right now," Sam pointed out.

Phyllis nodded, then said, "There is no try, only do or not do."

Sam laughed. "You're quotin' Yoda."

"I didn't know where it was from, I just knew I'd heard it. And it's certainly true in this case."

Not long after that, they reached the salon, having timed it so only five minutes remained until Phyllis's appointment. They went inside, where Aurora greeted them with a polite — but none too sincere, in Phyllis's opinion — smile.

"Good morning," the young woman said. Her two-toned hair was straight on both sides this morning, hanging down over her shoulders. She wore a tank top that left her arms bare and revealed more tattoos. "If you'll go on in, Mrs. Newsom, Courtney is ready for you."

She pointed to one of the stylists, a blonde around thirty.

Phyllis said, "Thank you. I suppose it's all right if my friend waits out here?"

"Of course. There are some copies of *Vogue* . . ."

Sam held up his paperback, smiled, and said, "Thanks, but I got my own readin' material to pass the time. Not many shoot-em-up stories in *Vogue,* I don't imagine."

Aurora gave him a more genuine smile and said, "Oh, I don't know. The fashion industry can get pretty vicious."

"Maybe I'll check 'em out, then."

He was off to a good start, Phyllis thought as she entered the salon's main room. If Sam could charm Aurora, there was no telling what he might find out.

Like the paint and body shop, the smell of chemicals was strong in the salon. Ironic that both places had that in common, Phyllis mused. The stylist named Courtney greeted her with a smile and said, "Mrs. Newsom? Sit right down and tell me what you'd like for me to do."

"Well, I was thinking it was time for a new look," Phyllis said. "I thought I'd just put myself in your hands. Your salon has a wonderful reputation."

"Pauline wouldn't have it any other way."

"Yes, I've heard that she's very devoted to making her clients happy." Phyllis had noted that Pauline didn't seem to be around this morning, which might mean her employees would be more liable to talk freely.

"We all feel that way," Courtney said. "Of course, you can't please everybody all the time."

"I know that. Do you ever have customers get angry at the way their hair turns out?"

"Sure. Not me, specifically, mind you." Courtney smiled. "Last year we had a woman get so mad she threatened to sue Pauline. Thank goodness I wasn't the one who took care of her."

"Who was?" Phyllis glanced around and lowered her voice to a conspiratorial tone. "Just so I'll know who I might not want working on my hair in the future, you know."

"Oh, that girl's not here anymore. In fact, she —" Courtney stopped short, then went on, "Never mind. Pauline doesn't like for us to talk about that. Let's talk about your hair, instead. When did you wash your hair last?"

"Yesterday morning."

"Did you use conditioner or any hair products?" Courtney asked.

"No, I just shampooed, blow dried, and

142

used the flat iron on some strays."

"Perfect. I'm thinking some highlights and maybe a different cut, something a little more . . . stylish . . ."

"Whatever you think, but remember, I'm not young anymore."

"Maybe not, but you've got great skin. Maybe you should get a facial next time you come in and make it even better."

"You know, that's a good idea. I wonder if it would be possible to work it in today."

"I don't know," Courtney said with a frown. "I can check for you, if you'd like."

The longer she could stay here talking to these people, the better, Phyllis thought. She nodded and said, "That would be great. Thank you."

Courtney stepped over to one of the other stations and talked briefly to the young black woman working there. She came back and reported to Phyllis, "Talia said she could work you in as soon as I'm finished with your hair."

"Thank you. I'm really grateful."

"Always happy to help."

How much of that was true and how much was just angling for a good tip was debatable, Phyllis thought, but she supposed it didn't really matter. The end result was what counted.

And she had already picked up some interesting information. She had a very strong hunch that the stylist who had angered a customer enough for the woman to threaten a lawsuit had been Roxanne Jackson. And that, in turn, must have angered Pauline. Phyllis could imagine Pauline lighting into Roxanne over the problem. Maybe Roxanne had taken offense, and the confrontation had escalated into an argument . . .

That was pure speculation, and flimsy speculation, at that. But it was one more possibility to add to the growing list in Phyllis's mind. Like most people, Roxanne had had problems in her life that, if taken to extremes, could provide a motive for murder. Phyllis had learned over the years that someone who supposedly got along with everybody and had no enemies was just good at covering up such things. She wasn't pleased that she had gotten so cynical, and she tried to guard against it, but she supposed that under the circumstances, it had been inevitable.

Courtney lightly spritzed Phyllis's hair and quickly trimmed her hair. Courtney explained how she would create fullness by cutting short feathered layers and wispy fringe giving her a soft but elegant style.

She started to work in the chemicals for the highlights], telling Phyllis that she was going to use two tones of brown to cover a little of the gray, but playing up her natural color. She used a brush to paint on the highlighter applying it on small sections of hair and then wrapping each setion in foil.

While that was going on, Phyllis tried again several times to steer the conversation back around to Roxanne, but Courtney sidestepped the questions and seemed determined not to say anything that might get Pauline angry at her.

When Courtney was finished for the moment, she said, "We'll need to let that sit for a while. I'm going to check on one of my other clients who is here for a bang trim, and I'll be back in a few minutes, okay?"

"Of course," Phyllis said. "I can't wait to see how this is going to look."

"I'm sure you're going to like it."

Courtney left her sitting in the chair with a plastic cape draped over her and walked to the other side of the salon.

"She's dead, you know."

The voice took Phyllis by surprise. She looked over at the woman sitting in the next chair. The woman was leaned back with some sort of creamy mask spread over her face. Her eyes were closed, but Phyllis was sure she was the one who had spoken.

"What?"

"She's dead. The girl who nearly caused Pauline to be sued. I can tell you all about it if you'd like."

Phyllis glanced around. None of the salon's employees were close by at the moment, and she wasn't going to pass up a chance for some gossip . . . especially when that gossip might be just what she needed to save Danny Jackson from a prison term he didn't deserve.

"I'd like that very much," Phyllis said as she leaned closer to her new-found friend.

CHAPTER 13

Out in the waiting area, Sam had opened his paperback, but he read only a few pages before looking up and asking Aurora, "You don't have a Coke machine in here, do you?"

She smiled again and said, "No, I'm afraid not. But I have a little fridge back here with bottled water if you'd like one."

"That sounds good. I'd be obliged to you."

Aurora turned her swivel chair around, reached under a counter where Sam couldn't see, and asked, "Regular, coconut, or vitamin-infused?"

"Oh, I think regular will do me just fine, thanks." He stood up and moved over to the desk so he could take the bottle of water she handed him. He unscrewed the cap, took a long swallow, and nodded. "Mighty good, even if it's not infused. Thanks again."

"Not a problem, Mr. Newsom."

"Oh, I'm not Mr. Newsom. Phyllis and I

are good friends, I guess you'd say. Fact is, we sort of live together." He waggled his bushy eyebrows, imitating Groucho Marx, who there was a good chance Aurora wasn't familiar with. He extended a hand and added, "Name's Sam Fletcher."

Aurora laughed at the eyebrow-wiggle, then shook his hand as she said, "I'm glad to meet you, Mr. Fletcher, and good for you."

Let her draw her own conclusions, Sam thought, as long as it made her friendly and willing to talk.

"This isn't the first beauty shop where I've waited for her," he went on, "but I reckon it's maybe the nicest."

"Oh, Paul's isn't a beauty shop. It's a *salon*. Hearing it called a beauty shop usually makes my aunt pretty mad, although she'll hold it in rather than risk offending a customer."

"Your aunt runs the place?"

"She owns it. Pauline Gibbs."

Sam nodded and said, "Yeah, come to think of it, I believe Phyllis mentioned somethin' about meetin' her the other day. She's not around?"

"No, she's gone to the bank to take care of some business."

"I know Phyllis was impressed with her.

Impressed with the whole place, to tell you the truth. She was sure pleased when you called yesterday and told her she could get in so soon."

"Well . . . that was Pauline's idea."

"Really? I thought somebody cancelled on y'all."

"They did," Aurora said, "but there were nine names on the list ahead of Mrs. Newsom's. Pauline told me to go ahead and call her, though. When I asked her why, she said we haven't been getting enough new customers lately. The other ladies on the cancellation list are all regular clients. They'll keep coming back. And if she's pleased, Mrs. Newsom will, too." The young woman shrugged. "I guess it makes sense."

"Unless those other ladies find out somebody got bumped ahead of 'em. They might not appreciate that."

Aurora leaned forward and looked around. She lowered her voice, even though there was no one to overhear, and said, "You won't tell anybody, will you? I shouldn't have said anything. I don't want to get in trouble —"

"Don't worry," Sam broke in, raising a hand to reassure her. "Beauty shop politics — I mean, beauty *salon* politics — is none of my business."

Aurora sat back and heaved a sigh of relief. "Sometimes I talk too much," she said. "Pauline doesn't like that, especially when it's about what goes on here at the salon."

"Well, you can understand her feelin' that way. She doesn't want anything hurtin' the business. I mean, Phyllis told me that somethin' happened to one of the young ladies who used to work here, and that must've caused a problem."

"You mean Roxanne."

Sam shook his head vaguely and said, "I dunno. I never really was sure what she was talkin' about."

Aurora glanced around again, evidently unable to suppress the urge to explain. Then she said, "There was a girl murdered, right here in the salon."

Sam opened his eyes wider. "You mean while ladies were gettin' their hair done?"

"No, no, it was in the evening, after the salon was closed. Roxanne was here working late, and her husband came in and killed her."

"That's terrible," Sam said.

"I know. Not that I really liked Roxanne all that much." She made a face. "She was sort of full of herself. Stuck up, you know. But Danny — her husband — he was a lot

150

nicer. I couldn't believe it when I heard what he did. I was always glad to see him when he stopped by to talk to Roxanne or to pick her up if her car wasn't running. He was pretty cute, too."

"I guess some murderers are."

Aurora blew out a breath and shook her head. "Anyway, it shook us all up pretty bad for a while, to think that it could happen right here where we work every day. And yeah, it hurt business for a while. But Pauline's customers really like how they're treated here, so eventually nearly all of them came back. By now it's like nothing ever happened. Some of the girls weren't even working here then, so it doesn't mean anything to them."

"This Roxanne, she was here by herself when it happened?"

"That's right." Aurora made a face again. "She was one of Pauline's favorites, I guess you could say. Pauline let her book some late appointments and close up when she was finished. She'd take the day's deposit to the bank when she did that."

"Sounds like she had her eye on runnin' the place one o' these days."

"Yeah, you might think so." Aurora frowned slightly. "Funny thing, though. Roxanne didn't act like she was trying to take over. Maybe a little, starting out, but there at the end it was more like she was counting the days until she got out of here. She never came right out and said it, but that was the impression I got."

"She must've had another job lined up."

"If she did, she never said anything about it. It was more like she was going to blow it all off, like she didn't need the job anymore." Aurora's eyes opened wider. "Or maybe she had a premonition of her own death!"

"That doesn't seem too likely," Sam said. "If she had, wouldn't she be worried or even scared?"

"Maybe. Or maybe it was such a strong premonition that she knew she couldn't do anything about it. Like . . . her time was up."

"Hard to believe."

"Oh, there are things out there we can't explain," Aurora said solemnly. "Lots of things.

Like pretty girls with blue and purple hair, Sam thought.

"Did you ever think that maybe it wasn't her husband who killed her?" he ventured.

"Oh, no, the cops caught him pretty much red-handed. I mean, he was the one who called 911, but he just did that to try to throw suspicion off of him. Don't you think?"

"I don't know," Sam said. "Remember, this is the first I've heard about the whole thing."

"Well, Danny was tried and found guilty and sent off to prison, I guess. Him being convicted was really the last I heard about it. So he wouldn't have been found guilty if he wasn't really guilty, would he?"

"I suppose not. Although you hear about that happenin' from time to time."

"Yeah, I guess so." She smiled. "Anyway, I need to get back to work. I have to call and confirm tomorrow's appointments. Wouldn't want my aunt to come in and find me not doing my job. But I've enjoyed talking to you, Mr. Fletcher."

"Likewise," Sam said. He went back to the comfortably upholstered bench, taking the bottle of water Aurora had given him. He sat down and opened his paperback again.

But even though he looked at the pages, his eyes didn't really focus on the words at first. He spent a few minutes thinking about what he had learned from the young woman. At first glance, it didn't amount to much, but in trying to solve a murder, little things often turned out to be important.

He glanced into the salon area, wondering how Phyllis was doing with her efforts.

"I'm Desiree Chilton," the woman in the next chair said.

"Phyllis Newsom," Phyllis introduced herself, hoping the woman wouldn't recognize her name.

"It's nice to meet you. And I have to agree you have really beautiful skin. I hope mine looks that good when I'm your age." Desiree gestured toward the cream spread all over her face. "That's one reason for this. And I hope I didn't offend you by mentioning your age . . . ."

"Not at all," Phyllis assured her. "I'm proud of every year I've spent on this earth."

"Well, that's a good way to be."

It was hard to tell with the mask she was wearing, but Phyllis figured Desiree was in her thirties. She had blond hair pulled back in a long ponytail. A cape covered most of her body, but Phyllis could see the expensive shoes she wore, along with part of the designer jeans. Evidently, Desiree had plenty of money, which is just what Phyllis would have expected from one of the salon's customers.

"Anyway," Desiree went on, "I was going to tell you about what happened to Roxanne, the poor girl. Her husband killed her right here in the salon. Beat her to death with his bare hands."

"Good Lord." Phyllis didn't have to fake the reaction. Even though she knew the alleged facts of the case quite well by now, hearing it stated so bluntly made it seem even more horrifying. "He came in and attacked her while people were here?"

"No, it was after hours, but Roxanne was still here. Her husband called the police, I guess because he knew he'd be the only real suspect, and tried to claim he'd found her that way, but of course no one believed him. I'm pretty sure he was found guilty at his trial, although I didn't really keep up with it."

"I guess you knew Roxanne pretty well," Phyllis said.

"She was the best! I always asked for her when I came in. It was devastating when I lost her!" Desiree sighed. "That sounded callous, didn't it? I didn't really mean it quite like that . . . but I could talk to her about almost anything, and it's certainly true that none of the other girls here have quite the same touch Roxanne did. Shelley Dawson is crazy."

"I don't know who that is," Phyllis said.

"Shelley? Oh, she got mad and pitched a

155

fit a week or so before Roxanne was killed. She claimed Roxanne butchered her hair. But if you ask me, it looked all right. And believe me, it takes a miracle worker to make Shelley's hair look even all right! She should have been thankful Roxanne did as good a job as she did. Instead, like I said, she caused all kinds of commotion and trouble by complaining to Pauline. Then of course Pauline got mad at Roxanne and it was just a big, unpleasant mess."

"That's terrible. Roxanne must have been pretty upset about the whole deal, too."

"You'd think so," Desiree said. "Really, though, she sort of just shrugged it off, like she didn't care all that much, even though Shelley wanted Pauline to fire her. It never came to that, of course, and then a week later . . . well, none of it mattered anymore because of what happened."

"The murder, you mean."

"That's right. Murder makes everything else sort of pale into insignificance, doesn't it?"

"It has a way of doing that, all right," Phyllis agreed.

"Anyway, that's the story, and that's why nobody around here likes to talk about it." Desiree sighed again. "I do miss Roxanne, though. I used to tell that girl everything! I mean, if you're going to trust somebody with something as important as your hair and face, you can trust them with anything, right?"

"I suppose so," Phyllis said.

"I'd better shut up now. That's hard for me to do, if you haven't guessed." She laughed. "Talia's going to fuss at me for taking a chance on cracking this mask . . ." Desiree's voice dropped to a whisper. "And she and Courtney are coming back."

The two stylists returned to their stations and went back to work on Phyllis and Desiree. Phyllis pretended to be paying attention to what Courtney was doing, but actually her mind was going over everything Desiree had said. The woman hadn't really given Phyllis any new information, as far as she could tell, but at the same time, something had started to stir in the back of her brain. It wasn't a coherent picture yet, or even close to that, but there *was* some sort of pattern that might be important, Phyllis sensed. She just couldn't tell what it was.

Maybe Sam had had better luck with Aurora, she thought.

CHAPTER 14

Phyllis tried to talk to Talia while the young woman was working on her face, but Talia was close-mouthed and discouraged conversation, saying, "You need to be still while I'm spreading this cream on, Mrs. Newsom. We need a nice, even layer."

"Of course," Phyllis said, careful to barely move her lips as she spoke.

Pauline came in while the mask was hardening on Phyllis's face. The salon owner emerged from a door in the rear of the room. Phyllis supposed she had either been back there in an office the whole time, or else she had just returned from somewhere and had come in through a rear door.

Pauline came over to her and said, "Mrs. Newsom! It's good to see you again." She smiled and patted Phyllis's cape-covered shoulder. "No, no, don't say anything. Wouldn't want y'all to risk ruinin' all of Talia's good work. Just give me a thumbs-up if you're bein' treated right."

Phyllis responded with the affirmative gesture.

"Good! If you have any problems, you just let me know, hear? We want all our clients at Paul's Beauty Salon to leave happy."

Unlike Shelly Dawson, Phyllis thought. The woman had been so upset that she'd wanted Roxanne fired, but that hadn't happened. It was 'way too farfetched to think that Shelley might have nursed her anger for a week and then come back to take it out on Roxanne, wasn't it?

Unfortunately, Phyllis knew that crazier things had happened. The very first case she'd solved had involved old grudges . . .

And just how angry had Pauline been at Roxanne over that flare-up, Phyllis wondered? She hadn't fired Roxanne, but according to Desiree Chilton, Roxanne might not have acted very grateful for that reprieve. Roxanne's attitude, on top of the other trouble, might have rubbed Pauline the wrong way . . .

Now she was just going around in circles, Phyllis told herself as she watched Pauline move along and talk to the other clients in the salon, laughing and complimenting and generally currying favor with them. She had seen bosses like that before, all sweetness and light when customers were around but the Dragon Lady when it was just the workers.

When Talia was finished, Phyllis suggested that she could use a manicure, too. She wanted to spend more time here, talk to more of the employees, although with Pauline around it was kind of doubtful how forthcoming they would be.

She would have even been willing to have a pedicure, although she didn't like people messing with her feet. She was too ticklish for that to be comfortable.

"You'll have to ask Pauline about that," Talia said. "I think all of our nail people may be booked solid for the day, though."

"It can't hurt to ask," Phyllis said. "And thank you for everything you did, Talia." She regarded herself in the mirror. "Not bad for an old lady."

Talia's natural expression seemed to be a solemn one, but she smiled slightly at that.

"You look really good, Mrs. Newsom," she said. "I hope you'll come back."

"I'm sure I will," Phyllis said . . . although what she was really sure of was that when she saw the bill for everything, she was going to have a hard time keeping her jaw from dropping.

But it was only money, she told herself.

That didn't count for as much when it was stacked up against Danny Jackson's life.

When Phyllis asked Pauline about a manicure and pedicure, the redhead smiled regretfully.

"I'm afraid we can't accommodate you for that today, Phyllis. But I'm sure Aurora would be glad to check the schedule and make an appointment for you as soon as possible."

"All right," Phyllis said. Like she had thought about the original appointment, she could always cancel it later on. "And thank you for getting me in so quickly for this appointment."

"We're always happy to have new customers. Y'all come back any time."

"I settle up with Aurora in front?"

"Yep."

Pauline was obviously ready to move on. Phyllis had stretched this out as long as she could. There wasn't anything else to be gained here, at least right now.

She opened one of the glass doors and stepped into the reception area. Sam must have seen her coming, because he was already on his feet, wearing a big grin on his face.

"Remember in those old cartoons how the wolf's eyes would bug out a foot in front of his face whenever he saw a pretty girl?" Sam said. "Well, that's sorta the way I feel right now."

"You look great, Mrs. Newsom," Aurora said with what sounded like genuine friendliness. Sam must have thawed out her attitude, Phyllis thought. "Those highlights in your hair really work."

"You're workin' it, all right," Sam said.

"Hush," Phyllis told him, but she smiled as she said it. She had left her purse with Sam. She got it now and took out her credit card.

Aurora announced the amount. Phyllis was braced for it and didn't gulp. She handed over the card. Aurora ran it, printed out a slip for Phyllis to sign, and stapled the duplicate to the bill she also printed out. It was all done very efficiently.

"I was talking to Pauline about a manicure and pedicure," Phyllis said as she handed back the pen and charge slip.

"Sure." Aurora consulted the schedule on her monitor. "How about next Thursday at one?"

"All right," Phyllis said, nodding.

Aurora wrote on an appointment card and handed it to her. "There you go," the young woman said. "And you really do look nice."

"Thank you," Phyllis said. She smiled,

then went out the front door while Sam held it open for her.

As they walked toward the pickup, Phyllis went on, "Now that we're outside, you can tell me how it really looks. The hair is ridiculous on a woman my age, isn't it?"

"Not hardly," Sam said. "Every word I said in there was the truth. You look like a million bucks."

"A million dollars isn't worth what it once was."

"It's still a whole heap of money to me. And you're worth more than that, as far as I'm concerned."

Sam opened the pickup door for her, and then, when he had gone around and climbed behind the wheel, Phyllis said, "Looks aside, how did it go with Aurora?"

"Seems like a nice girl. A little on the dizzy side, maybe, but not too much. You were right about her not likin' Roxanne, though. I wouldn't say they were out-and-out enemies, but Aurora didn't have much use for her, that's for sure. Said she was stuck-up and that she was Pauline's favorite. That rubbed Aurora the wrong way, seein' as how Pauline's her aunt."

"She is?" Phyllis said. "I didn't know that. Neither of them mentioned it the other day." She paused and thought for a moment, then asked, "What about Danny? Did Aurora say anything about him?"

Sam started the pickup and backed out of the parking space. As he pulled forward, he said, "Accordin' to Aurora, Danny was cute."

"So she *did* like him."

"That doesn't mean she ever made a play for him and made Roxanne jealous."

"But she might have."

Sam frowned and said, "I don't think so. Wouldn't surprise me if she flirted some with him. And if he'd flirted back hard enough . . ." Sam took a hand off the wheel and wiggled it. "Maybe. You got to remember, I don't know Danny at all. I don't know how he would've reacted in a case like that. Could be he's the one who made a pass at Aurora, if there was a pass."

"I don't suppose I really know him well enough to say for sure, either," Phyllis mused. "I haven't spend much time around him since he was in high school. Hardly any, in fact."

"So we can't rule out the idea that somethin' was goin' on between Danny and Aurora."

"But we don't have any evidence that it was, either." Phyllis thought for a moment. "You said Roxanne was Pauline's favorite?"

"Aurora seemed to think so, anyway."

"Something happened a week or so before Roxanne was killed that makes me think the relationship may have changed," Phyllis said. She told Sam about the complaint against Roxanne lodged by Shelley Dawson. "From what the stylist I was talking to told me, it turned into a huge uproar. The woman even threatened to sue the salon. That must have really upset Pauline. But Roxanne didn't seem to care that much."

"Now that goes right along with somethin' else Aurora told me," Sam said as he drove around a high, curving ramp that led onto Interstate 30. "She thought Roxanne had sorta lost interest in the salon, too. She'd started out workin' hard, like she was ambitious and even had her eye on managin' the place for Pauline someday, but then she got to where she was just markin' time."

"Courtney felt the same way about her. But what would make Roxanne act like that? And could it have anything to do with why she was killed?"

"Figure out the first question and you might have the answer to the second," Sam said.

Phyllis had been in the salon for quite a

while, so once again they stopped for lunch on the way back to Weatherford. Even though they weren't really hungry anymore, the aroma in the air when they got home and stepped into the kitchen was enough to make their mouths start to water.

"Lord have mercy," Sam breathed. "That smells *good.*"

"Oh, my, it does," Phyllis agreed.

Carolyn came into the kitchen and said, "You're back." Then she stopped short and looked at Phyllis without saying anything.

When the suspense got to be too much, Phyllis said, "Well? What do you think?"

"It's very nice," Carolyn said, then added, "It might be a little bit *young* for you."

"Nonsense," Eve said as she walked into the kitchen, too. "It looks spectacular, dear. Why, it's taken years off your look."

"Better than years off your life," Sam said. "What's that I'm smellin'?"

Phyllis was grateful to him for changing the subject, although she knew he was genuinely curious about the source of that delicious aroma. She was, too.

"It's a slab pie. A chocolate cherry slab pie to be precise.," Carolyn explained. "This is the recipe I'm going to send in to the contest, if it turns out the way I hope."

"I don't have a clue what a slab pie is, but

judgin' by the smell, it's gonna turn out mighty good," Sam declared.

Phyllis was relieved to know what Carolyn's contest recipe was at last. She didn't want to step on her old friend's toes with the idea she'd had. She said, "I'm sure it'll be wonderful. I was thinking about doing my column for the issue when the contest results come out about fruit pies. I've had an idea for a berry pie in the back of my mind for a while now."

"What sort of berries?" Sam asked.

"I was thinking maybe blackberries and blueberries."

Carolyn frowned and said, "That sounds a little violent, don't you think?"

"How can a pie be violent?" Eve asked.

"I mean, black and blue berries? Especially when you're investigating a murder where someone was beaten to death?"

"That never occurred to me," Phyllis said.

"I think it's quite a stretch, myself," Eve said. "Anyway, that issue of the magazine won't come out for, what, three or four months? By then the murder will be long since solved and the real culprit will have been brought to justice."

"We hope," Phyllis said.

"I don't think anyone doubts your abilities, dear."

Maybe not, Phyllis thought, but having people depending on her when it was a matter of life and death was a considerable responsibility. A lot more important than pie recipes, that was for sure. Carolyn's efforts had sparked her creativity, though, and after competing with Carolyn for so many years when it came to cooking, sometimes it was difficult for Phyllis to remember that those days were behind her now.

She turned to Carolyn and said, "I think the pie smells delicious, and I definitely want a sample when it's done and has a chance to cool off."

"Me, too," Sam said. "Not too cool, though. It's still got to be warm enough to melt the ice cream a little."

"How can you judge a pie properly if you cover it with ice cream?" Carolyn asked.

"That's the good thing about it. I'm not judgin' it. I'm just eatin' it."

CHAPTER 15

Something else had occurred to Phyllis during the drive back from Fort Worth, an angle she hadn't explored yet on this case. More and more, people put their whole lives on display on social media, and once those posts were online, for the most part they stayed there forever. She wasn't that familiar with some of the platforms, but she knew her way around Facebook and knew that it had become popular while Mike was in college. People in his generation still used it extensively.

That included Danny, of course, so after sitting down at the computer, she went to Facebook and searched for him.

Finding him took several minutes. There were a *lot* of Danny Jacksons. But his page hadn't been deleted, and when she found it, Phyllis began scanning down through the posts.

The page wasn't private, and the most

recent post was a few days before Roxanne's murder. Not surprisingly, the page hadn't been updated since then. The posts were innocuous, though. Many of them were reposts of humorous memes. Danny had an interest in hot rods, since there were some videos of racing. The more personal posts were usually about places he and Roxanne had gone or things they had done together, often including smiling photographs of her. If there was any indication of trouble between the two of them, it wasn't apparent to Phyllis.

There were a few pictures of the paint and body shop and Brian Flynn, Danny's business partner. One of them showed the two men with their arms around each other's shoulders, grinning proudly into the camera. Judging by the date, Phyllis figured that was when the shop had opened. Roxanne had probably taken the picture.

Phyllis studied Danny's page for quite a while before admitting to herself that she wasn't going to find anything worthwhile here. All it did was support Danny's claim that he loved his wife and wouldn't have hurt her.

Maybe there would be a different story on Roxanne's page, if it was still there, Phyllis thought as she began to search for it.

Unfortunately, it appeared that Roxanne's page had been deleted, if indeed she had had one. She was listed as his wife in his profile information, but it wasn't an active link. She wasn't tagged in any of Danny's posts that mentioned her or pictures that included her, so that was an indication she didn't have a page of her own. There were still people who weren't on Facebook. Plenty in Phyllis's generation, in fact, but some among younger folks, too.

She searched Twitter, Snapchat, and Instagram for Roxanne Jackson and didn't find anything, then it occurred to her that she didn't know what Roxanne's last name had been before she married Danny. Some women continued to use their maiden name, and that could be true on social media as well.

She would have to find out about that, but in the meantime she went back to Facebook and decided to look up some of the other people involved in the case. She started with Brian Flynn.

Again there were a number of people with that name, but within a few minutes Phyllis was able to find the right one and start backtracking through his posts. Brian had been pretty active on Facebook, reposting and sharing quite a few links to funny video clips and car-related topics. Like Danny, he had a clear fondness for hot rods and racing. Being a single man, however, Brian had posted numerous pictures of pretty girls, often scantily clad, draping themselves across the fenders of cars. Some were risque enough to make Phyllis blush.

She noticed a gap in the dates of the posts and realized that it had occurred right after Roxanne's murder. That made sense. The wife of his best friend had been murdered, and that best friend had been arrested for the crime. That was enough to make anybody forget about Facebook for a few days.

Phyllis dug deeper and saw that Danny had liked and commented on a number of Brian's posts. That wasn't surprising, either. Danny had disappeared from Brian's timeline after the murder, of course, since he was in jail.

Then a black-and-white photo caught Phyllis's eye. Brian hadn't posted it. Someone named Roger Terrill had, but evidently he was friends with Brian because Brian was tagged in the post, causing it show up on his timeline. Phyllis could tell right away that the photograph had been scanned from an old high school yearbook. It showed three football players, in uniform but with their helmets off, standing on the sidelines of a football field, each with his arm around a pretty cheerleader who snuggled against him. All six people in the photo were smiling with the cheerful confidence of youth.

Phyllis clicked on the picture to enlarge it and leaned forward to study it more intently. There was a caption under the photo identifying the teenagers in it. Phyllis didn't need the caption to recognize Brian Flynn. The resemblance between the younger version of Brian and the way he looked now was unmistakable.

The girl he had his arm around looked familiar, too. Phyllis's gaze dropped to the caption and she caught her breath.

"Whatcha doin'?" Sam asked from behind her.

She straightened in the chair in front of the desk where the computer and monitor sat. Her finger pointed at the photograph on the screen.

"That's Brian Flynn when he was in high school," Phyllis said. "And look who his girlfriend is."

Sam bent down to peer over her shoulder. He said, "Is that . . . ?"

"Her name in the caption is Roxanne Macrae," Phyllis said. "But that's her, no doubt about it. That's Danny's wife."

Armed with Roxanne's maiden name, Phyllis began searching again. She still didn't find a Facebook page under that name, but she was able to determine that Roxanne Macrae had graduated from Western Hills High School the same year as Brian Flynn — which was also the same year Mike and Danny had graduated from Weatherford.

"You know, just because a football player has his arm around a cheerleader in a yearbook picture doesn't mean they're boyfriend and girlfriend," Sam pointed out. "Pictures like that are staged all the time."

"I suppose that's true," Phyllis said. "But look at the caption: *Lovebirds.* The conclusion is pretty inescapable. Even if the picture *was* just staged for the yearbook, though, that doesn't change the fact that Brian knew Roxanne from high school. In fact . . ." The wheels in Phyllis's brain were starting to revolve faster now. "When we were talking to Brian, he referred to Roxanne as 'Roxie'. That implies a certain degree of familiarity, doesn't it? I don't recall Danny referring to her that way, or anyone else we've talked to about this case."

"Danny didn't use that name while you

were talkin' to him in jail," Sam said. "He might've around friends, though, like Brian."

Phyllis nodded. "That's true. You know what we're going to have to do."

"Ask him?"

"That's right."

"Before you do that . . . if you're right and the two of 'em dated in high school, it doesn't necessarily have to have anything to do with what happened to Roxanne."

Phyllis knew Sam was playing devil's advocate now, and she was grateful for that. Any theory she might form had to be tested over and over again, until there was no doubt in her mind that it was correct.

"The whole thing could be a coincidence," Sam went on. "Maybe Brian and Roxanne dated in high school, and then didn't see each other for years, until Danny married her and introduced her to Brian like the two of 'em had never met before. I can sure see why both of 'em would keep quiet about that and not say anything to Danny, especially if things were serious between 'em back in the day."

"You mean if they slept together."

"That could be a mite uncomfortable," Sam said. "For all three of them."

Phyllis sat back in the chair, her excitement ebbing a little. She had thought she was on to something, but Sam could be right. The whole thing could amount to an embarrassing coincidence, nothing more.

"You're right, but it still won't hurt anything to find out for certain about the Roxie business."

"It sure won't," Sam said.

Phyllis took out her phone and called Jimmy D'Angelo. She couldn't just call the jail in Fort Worth and ask Danny a question, but as his lawyer, D'Angelo might be able to.

When the attorney came on the phone, he said, "I'm glad you called, Phyllis. I was just wondering how you and Sam were coming along with the investigation."

"We've come across several things that *might* be related to Roxanne's murder, but nothing that we can prove had anything to do with it."

"I'm sorry to hear that. I just got word that Danny's going to be transferred to Huntsville next Tuesday."

"That's less than a week from now," Phyllis said. She felt the pressure increasing, like a vise tightening. It had to be a lot worse than that for Danny.

"He's been lucky it hasn't happened before now," D'Angelo said. "So if you're

176

going to come up with anything . . ."

"You don't have to tell me. It needs to be soon. Actually, I called because there's something you might be able to help out on. Can you get Danny on the phone?"

"Sure I can. I'm his lawyer. It might take a little while, but I can do it. Do you need me to ask him something?"

"Yes," Phyllis said. "Ask him if he ever called his wife Roxie."

D'Angelo was silent for a moment, then said, "You mean, like a pet name for her or something like that?"

"Exactly."

"And this is important to the case?"

"It could be."

D'Angelo hesitated again, but only for a second. "All right. I'm curious, but I won't ask you to explain right now. I'll just take your word for it. You want me to call you back as soon as I find out anything?"

"That would be fine."

"Okay. You'll hear from me later this afternoon, I hope. Or possibly in the morning. But as soon as I know anything, you will, too."

"Thank you, Mr. D'Angelo."

"Not a problem. In the meantime . . ."

"I'll keep looking," Phyllis promised.

"That's what I like to hear. So long."

Phyllis broke the connection and looked again at the yearbook picture of Brian Flynn and Roxanne Macrae. Their smiles were big and genuine, she thought, the smiles of two people in love.

Just like Roxanne and Danny had looked in their pictures.

Was one of those things a lie . . . and had it led to murder?

CHAPTER 16

Phyllis knew that when she had too much information whirling around inside her head, one of the best things she could do was to get away from it completely for a while. To that end, she turned off the computer monitor and retreated to the kitchen, where Carolyn had taken her chocolate cherry slab pie out of the oven and set it on the counter to cool. The smell wafting from it was still delicious.

"Oh my, that is enormous."

Carolyn and Eve were sitting at the table drinking coffee. "I know. It took eight cups of flour just for the crust, but wouldn't that be great for a party? I saw one in a magazine and I just had to try it."

Eve asked, "Where's Sam?"

"He went upstairs," Phyllis said. She smiled. "It's getting on toward his nap time. In fact, it's probably a little past it."

"We could cut the pie while he's sleeping," Carolyn suggested with an uncharacti-cally mischievous gleam in her eyes.

"Deprive Sam of fresh pie?" Eve asked. "He'd never forgive you!"

Phyllis poured herself a cup of coffee and sat down with them. "Well, it's not like we could eat the whole thing." She didn't want to think about the case, so she steered the conversation to less grim topics. Eve was still full of stories about Hollywood, and she was glad to share more of them.

If Phyllis had expected any blinding revelations to come on her, she would have been disappointed. Nothing else regarding the case had occurred to her by the time Sam came downstairs and joined them, sniffing the air.

"I think that pie smells like it's just about ready to cut," he said.

"You can tell that by the way it smells?" Carolyn asked.

"Well . . . that and the way my stomach's ready for it. Wait . . . that's a pie?" He leaned slightly over the counter, looked down at the pie, pointed a finger at his midsection, and said in an odd accent, "Get in ma belly!"

Carolyn and Eve looked at Phyllis, who shook her head and said, "I'm not even go-ing to ask."

Carolyn stood up, made shooing motions at Sam, and said, "Get away from that pie. I'll cut it. Although it's really too close to supper time to be eating pie."

"We'll eat light," Sam said. "Don't forget the ice cream."

Carolyn rolled her eyes and opened a drawer to get out a knife.

To her apparent disgust, not only Sam but also Phyllis and Eve scooped ice cream onto their slices. "This is wonderful," Phyllis proclaimed after a couple of bites.

"It certainly is," Eve declared. "You couldn't find anything better at Schwab's Drugstore in Hollywood. That's where Lana Turner was discovered, you know."

"Mighty good," Sam chimed in. "You're gonna win that contest for sure, Carolyn."

"I don't know about that," she said, then admitted, "It is pretty good, isn't it?"

Phyllis had finished and was wondering just how undignified it would be to pick up the saucer and lick it, when the doorbell rang. She knew Sam was thinking about licking his saucer, too, only he was liable to do it. She stood up and said, "I'll see who that is."

As she went into the living room, she looked through the front window and saw the sheriff's department car parked at the curb. As always, that sight prompted a mixture of emotions inside her. The first thought that came to mind was that Mike had stopped by, and that pleased her.

But that was followed inevitably by the possibility that something had happened to him, and someone had come to notify her. She knew he was in a profession that wasn't dangerous most of the time — Mike liked to tell her about deputies he served with who had never drawn their guns in the line of duty, during long careers — but it could turn that way at any second, with little or no warning. That situation had grown worse in recent years, and so there was a low-level dread always present in the back of Phyllis's mind when it came to her son's safety.

Because of that, a wave of relief went through Phyllis when she opened the door and saw Mike standing there on the porch, apparently hale and hearty.

He had a worried frown on his face, though, instead of his normally cheerful expression, and that instantly made Phyllis worry, too.

"What's wrong, Mike?" she said as she stepped back to let him into the house. She knew she didn't have to ask him in.

He followed her into the foyer and said, "It's Sarah's mom. She's in the hospital."

"Oh, dear. Is it serious?"

"They don't know yet," Mike said with a shake of his head. "They're running tests. But Sarah wants to go out to California to see her."

"Well, of course she does. Having lost her father, she's bound to be really worried about her mother."

Sarah's father had passed away about a year and a half earlier. At the time, Sarah had tried to talk her mother into moving back to Texas so she would be closer, but the woman wouldn't hear of it. She'd been determined to continue living in California on her own. Although Phyllis had commiserated with her daughter about that, secretly she admired the decision. It took courage to live alone after having been in a long marriage. She knew that from experience. She hadn't been able to do it, herself, but had rented out rooms in the big old house after Kenny's death and created a surrogate family in Carolyn, Eve, and Sam.

Mike went on, "The thing is, she wants me to go with her. She's really scared that she's going to lose her mom, too. I don't know if it's really that serious, but it could be, I guess."

"Can you get the time off?"

"Yeah, I've got some personal days coming. That won't be a big problem. But . . ."

"Bobby," Phyllis said.

Mike made a face and said, "He just started kindergarten a few weeks ago, and he loves it. Sure, it wouldn't do any real harm to pull him out for a few days, and I wouldn't hesitate to do it if I thought the situation called for it, but at this point we really don't know much."

"You want to know if he can stay here."

"It's a lot to ask —"

"No, it's not," Phyllis said. "This is what family is for, to step in and help whenever it's needed. Of course I can look after him. *We* can look after him," she added, knowing that the others would pitch in, too. "But if it does turn out to be serious . . ."

"Then I'll fly back here and get him, so he can see his other grandma one more time. I hope. Life doesn't always give us those options. Anyway, that's the way things stand now. If you're sure you don't mind . . ."

Phyllis shook her head and said, "Of course not." Another thought occurred to her. "Have you talked about this with Sarah, though? She might prefer that you take Bobby with you now."

"It was actually her idea that Bobby stay with you if you were all right with it. She doesn't want to disrupt school for him, either. Don't worry, we talked it all out and we're in agreement." Mike smiled. "Anyway, you know how Sarah feels about you. She'd always trust Bobby with you, any time, anywhere. You're almost as much her mom as her actual mom is."

"I'm glad she feels that way. She's like a daughter to me, too."

"Now that that's settled . . . is that fresh pie I smell?"

"It's Carolyn's," Phyllis said with a smile. "Come on in the kitchen. I'll cut you a slice."

"Ohhh, you don't know how much I really want to. But there's not time. I need to get home, help Sarah round up everything Bobby will need, and then get him back over here. Then we'll have to head for the airport and catch a flight this evening."

"All right. I'd promise to save a piece for you, for when you get back, but with Sam in the house . . ."

Mike grinned and said, "I understand." He leaned closer and kissed her cheek. "Thanks, Mom." He turned toward the door, then stopped abruptly. "I almost forgot! What about Danny?"

"I'm still working on the case," Phyllis said. "There's nothing really solid to go on yet, but since you're here . . . do you remember ever hearing Danny refer to his wife as Roxie?"

"Roxie?" Mike repeated, his forehead creasing in a frown. "Nooo, I don't think so. He always called her Roxanne when he mentioned her to me. But maybe that's what he called her when they were alone, like I call Sarah — Never mind."

"Yes, you can keep whatever that is between the two of you," Phyllis said.

"What does that have to do with the murder?"

"Probably nothing. Just a little puzzle. The two of them met in college, didn't they?"

"That's right. Danny didn't like college much. Said the only worthwhile thing he got out of it was a pretty wife."

"So they weren't high school sweethearts or anything like that," Phyllis said, even though she already knew that wasn't the case.

"No, Roxanne went to high school over in Fort Worth somewhere, I think. She wasn't a Weatherford girl."

"All right."

"When we've got more time," Mike said, "you're going to explain all this to me. I might be able to help, since I *do* work in law enforcement and all. Although by the time we get back, you'll probably have the case solved."

Phyllis thought about Danny Jackson's impending transfer to the state penitentiary at Huntsville and hoped Mike was right about that.

When Mike was gone, she went back into the kitchen, where her friends were still sitting with empty pie saucers and coffee cups in front of them. Sam's saucer was clean enough she knew he had given in to the impulse to lick every last bit off of it.

"We weren't eavesdropping —" Carolyn began.

"Yes, we were," Eve said.

"— but we couldn't help overhearing some of that," Carolyn went on doggedly. "Bobby's coming to stay for a few days, isn't he?"

"That's right."

Sam said, "Well, I hope Sarah's mom turns out to be okay, but I'm always glad to have that little fella around. He's got a whole heap more energy than I do, so he and Buck can chase each other around the backyard until they're both worn out. I don't mind takin' him to school in the mornin', either, and pickin' him up afterward."

"I appreciate that," Phyllis told him. "I

know having a child here can be hard on the peace and quiet we're all used to."

"Peace and quiet's overrated," Sam said.

"Anyway, you're trying to solve a murder," Eve added. "That's not exactly peaceful."

And now she would have to do it with a very active six-year-old grandson underfoot, Phyllis thought. That would be an even bigger challenge.

She hoped she would be up to it.

CHAPTER 17

Jimmy D'Angelo called late that afternoon while Phyllis and Carolyn were putting supper together. They decided to keep it simple with tacos. Since they all ate pie earlier, Carolyn wanted a gluten-free supper since her arthritis was acting up.] Phyllis answered her cell phone, eager to learn what the lawyer had found out even though her earlier conversation with Mike had given her a pretty good idea what to expect.

"Took me a little while, but I was able to get Danny on the phone," the lawyer began. "I asked him what you wanted, about whether or not he ever called his wife Roxie, and he said he didn't. He told me he called her that one time, back when they were dating, and she asked him not to. Said it reminded her of a time in her life and things she'd rather forget."

"Well, that's interesting," Phyllis said. "So

she had some sort of past, despite being young."

"Hey, who among us doesn't?" D'Angelo said. "What's this all about? Danny was curious, but I put him off until I'd talked to you."

Phyllis had walked along the hallway from the kitchen toward the living room as she talked to the lawyer. She said quietly, "Brian Flynn lied about not knowing Roxanne before Danny married her. Well, not lied, really, but he didn't say anything about knowing her and that's a lie by omission, isn't it? Anyway, as it turns out, they were high school sweethearts."

D'Angelo let out a low whistle of surprise and asked, "You can prove that?"

"Yes. There are yearbook pictures of the two of them together, and I'm sure if you asked people they went to school with, they could confirm it."

In a musing tone, D'Angelo said, "So maybe Brian wanted to start things up again with Roxanne, and she wasn't having any of it. That could have led to an argument. Or maybe they did have something going on, and Roxanne wanted to break it off and tell Danny. That would ruin the business partnership, not to mention the friendship, between Danny and Brian."

"Those scenarios occurred to me as well," Phyllis said. "Brian had to know where Roxanne worked. While Danny was working late at the paint and body shop, Brian could have gone there to confront her, for whatever reason, and things got out of hand."

"She would have let him into the salon, I'll bet," D'Angelo said, his voice quickening with excitement. "After all, she'd known him for years. She wouldn't be expecting any trouble from him. That's how he was able to get close enough to knock her out with one punch." He paused. "This does us no good unless we can come up with something to put Brian on the scene that night. But if we can prove that's true and that the cops overlooked it, that might be enough to get Danny's conviction overturned and create reasonable doubt in a new trial."

"It's a trail to follow and see where it leads," Phyllis said. "And we can keep following up on some other things, too."

"Sounds good. I knew you could do this, Phyllis."

"I haven't done anything yet," she cautioned.

"It's just a matter of time. You want me to ask Danny how his wife and Brian got along? Maybe he noticed something suspicious?"

Phyllis thought about it for a second, then said, "No, not yet. Danny's already under a lot of stress. There's no point in giving him something else to worry about when it might turn out to be nothing."

"Okay." D'Angelo laughed. "I'm supposed to be the kid's lawyer, but here I am askin' you what to do. Must be the fact that you were a schoolteacher. Back where I went to school, the nuns were the last word on everything. I figure God sometimes asked *them* for advice, instead of the other way around."

"Well, of course, whatever you think is best —"

"No, no, I'm good with that. We've got a little time to play with yet."

But only a little, Phyllis thought as she said goodbye.

A short time after that, Mike and Sarah showed up with Bobby.

"Where's Buck?" the youngster asked as soon as he was in the door.

"Out in the backyard," Sam told him, pointing with a thumb toward the rear of the house. "You want to go see him?"

"Sure!"

The two of them headed down the hall in that direction while Mike set a small suitcase

192

on one of the chairs in the living room and Sarah gave Phyllis a hug.

"I can't thank you enough for looking after him," Sarah told her mother-in-law.

"We're happy to do it," Phyllis assured her. "You have plenty on your mind right now. You need to be able to go see about your mother without having to worry about anything else. Have you heard any more than when Mike was here earlier?"

"She was having chest pains bad enough to send her to the emergency room, and they put her right into the hospital. The last I heard, they were doing tests, trying to see if it's her heart or something else."

"Well, she'll be in our prayers, dear. You all will. Just let us know what's going on, and don't worry about Bobby."

"Thank you." Sarah hugged her again, then said to Mike, "Let's go say goodbye to him."

"It's gonna be rough being away from the little fella," Mike said. "At least it's not the first time."

A couple of years earlier, an ear infection had prevented Bobby from flying when his parents went to California to see Sarah's father. He had stayed with Phyllis then, and he had spent nights here in the old house on several other occasions.

Phyllis followed her son and daughter-in-law onto the back porch. Bobby was out in the yard in the fading light, throwing one of Buck's rope toys around while Sam watched from the porch. The Dalmatian raced after the toy every time, grabbing it and running around to keep it away from Bobby. The boy had to chase the dog to retrieve the toy and throw it again. Both of them seemed to be having a great time.

Bobby ran back over to the porch when Sarah called him. He started to get a little tearful when it sunk in on him that his parents were leaving him here and going somewhere without him. That was tempered by the fact that he would get to stay with his grandmother, Sam, Carolyn, Eve, and Buck.

"Will I still go to school?" he asked.

"One of us will take you and pick you up every day," Phyllis promised.

"Probably me," Sam added. "And I might just bring ol' Buck with me when I come to pick you up."

"So the kids at school can see him?" Bobby asked, brightening up a little.

"That's right."

"That'd be cool!"

He hugged Mike and Sarah goodbye, then stayed out in the yard with Sam and Buck while the others went back inside.

"Oh, this is hard," Sarah said. "But I think it'll be better all around, at least until we find out more."

"The important thing is to do whatever you can for your mother and let us take care of things here," Phyllis told her.

Mike said, "I wish this hadn't come up while you're dealing with that business about Danny."

"It'll be all right." Phyllis smiled. "I've learned how to multi-task."

And if any situation fell into that category, it would have to be taking care of her grandson and solving a murder at the same time!

Bobby ate supper with them after Mike and Sarah were gone. Tacos turned out the perfect choice since they were one of Bobby's favorites. Carolyn even made some guacamole to go with them since he loved it so much.

After supper, Sam offered to play a board game with Bobby. That freed up Phyllis to do some more online research concerning the case.

Newspaper archives yielded a number of sports section stories about high school football games in which Brian Flynn had played. He'd been the quarterback, and evidently quite a good one. But he had been injured in the last game of his senior year. There were no mentions of him playing in college or even being offered college scholarships, so Phyllis thought he'd probably been hurt badly enough that it ended his playing career.

That must have been quite a letdown, to be so close to potential success, only to have it taken away through no fault of your own.

Phyllis had hoped to find more photographs showing Brian and Roxanne together, but she wasn't able to locate any. Still, the one yearbook photo was enough, as far as she was concerned.

There was nothing else online about Brian. Like most people, it seemed that he'd led an unremarkable life.

Phyllis hadn't ruled out some connection between Roxanne's job and her death, so she searched for mentions of Pauline Gibbs, too. That turned up nothing. Phyllis cast her memory back, came up with the name of the woman who had been upset about the way Roxanne cut her hair, and searched for Shelley Dawson.

That produced quite a few results, mostly mentions in newspaper stories about various business deals and society functions in

Fort Worth. She was married to Arthur Dawson, and evidently they were partners in a very successful commercial real estate company. They had handled the development of several high-end shopping centers in some of Fort Worth's best areas. Phyllis wondered fleetingly if the Dawsons might have some connection to the planned housing development out by the farm house owned by Danny and Roxanne Jackson, but there was no mention in any of the stories about them being involved in residential real estate.

There were, however, several photographs of them at various black-tie affairs, usually sitting at tables with other expensively dressed couples. The Dawsons both appeared to be in their forties. Arthur was a handsome, dark-haired man, while Shelley, in a less charitable era, would have been described as horse-faced. She wore clothes and jewelry well, though, and her fair hair looked to be stylishly cut as far as Phyllis could tell. She wasn't as unattractive as Desiree Chilton had made her sound, although her husband was definitely the better-looking member of the couple.

Then Phyllis found another picture of them and frowned slightly in surprise. This photograph had been taken at some ballroom or banquet, too, but they weren't sitting at a table this time. Arthur Dawson was standing in front of an ornate fountain, and next to him, seated in a wheelchair, was Shelley. Her husband's left hand rested on her right shoulder as they both smiled at the camera.

Earlier, Phyllis had toyed with the idea that Shelley Dawson might have been so angry over what she regarded as a bad haircut that she had gone to the salon and gotten into an altercation with Roxanne, an argument that had turned fatal. That seemed awfully unlikely now. Roxanne might have opened the door and let Shelley into the building, but how could Shelley have mustered up the physical ability to beat another human being to death?

Phyllis checked the date on the photograph of Shelley in the wheelchair. It had been taken more than a year earlier. She might have been in the chair because of some sort of injury, Phyllis thought, an injury she had totally recovered from by the time Roxanne was killed.

But the photograph had been taken at a benefit auction to raise funds for muscular dystrophy research, Phyllis saw, and a quick check of the other stories about the couple revealed that the Dawsons seemed to be heavily involved with that charity. Probably because Shelley had been stricken with the disease herself but hadn't let that stop her from having a successful career in business. Phyllis found another newspaper article about her that went into detail about that very subject. Shelley had been unable to walk by the time she was twenty-five years old.

That ruled her out as a possible suspect. There was still a faint possibility that the threatened lawsuit had angered Pauline Gibbs enough to cause another argument between her and Roxanne, but Phyllis sensed that this whole line of inquiry was slipping away from her. Her instincts told her she was going to have to look elsewhere to find Roxanne's killer.

Carolyn came into the living room and said, "I've never seen a more cutthroat game of Chutes and Ladders in my life."

Phyllis looked over her shoulder. "You mean Sam and Bobby?"

"That's right. They're playing at the kitchen table."

"Is Sam letting him win?"

"Not as far as I could tell. That man is too competitive for that."

Phyllis hid a smile. *Pot, kettle. Kettle, pot,* she thought. No one was more competitive than Carolyn when it came to her recipes. Of course, Phyllis reminded herself, she had gotten caught up in the thrill of a cooking contest quite a few times herself . . .

She looked at the clock and said, "It's almost Bobby's bedtime. They're going to have to finish soon or else suspend the game until tomorrow night."

"I'll go and tell them that if somebody wins not to start another game."

"Thanks. I'll be in there in a minute."

Phyllis turned back to the computer and started closing down her searches. She wished all of life's problems could be closed down as easily. Just click on an "X" in the corner, and it was gone.

Or in this case, thinking about Brian Flynn and Roxanne Macrae Jackson, was it "Ex" . . . ?

Maybe tomorrow would bring the answer.

CHAPTER 18

Bobby had inherited a lot of his traits from Mike, including a reluctance to get out of bed in the morning and go to school. However, rousting a youngster from the covers and getting him up and moving proved to be like the old proverb about riding a bike, Phyllis discovered: once you knew how, you never really forgot.

When Bobby was good and awake, he was actually eager to go, since he liked kindergarten. After breakfast he piled into the pickup with Sam, and they headed for school.

Phyllis got dressed while Sam was gone. He wasn't back yet when she walked into the kitchen and found Carolyn and Eve sitting at the table and nursing second cups of coffee.

"I guess you're going out to investigate that murder again today," Carolyn said.

"I am . . . but if I have time, I might stop

by the store and pick up some things for that black and blueberry pie."

"You know," Eve said, "I have a friend who grows berries. She and her husband live between here and Springtown and have whole fields of berries. They would probably let us pick some fresh ones."

"Would there still be any this late in the season?" Phyllis asked. Fresh fruit was always better than canned or frozen.

"Well, I wouldn't know about that myself, of course, but I could find out."

"I'd appreciate it. We could have a little berry-picking expedition this weekend. Bobby might enjoy that."

"Goodness," Carolyn said. "I haven't picked berries in years. We used to when I was a little girl. We went and picked up pecans, too. I remember filling up bushel baskets with them!"

"It was fun, too, wasn't it?" Phyllis said.

"It was work, all that bending over . . . but I remember enjoying it," Carolyn admitted. She frowned. "Not picking cotton, though. I never enjoyed picking cotton."

"I can certainly agree with you on that," Phyllis said.

Sam came back in a short time later. Smiling, he said, "That kid sure loves to talk. He barely shut up the whole way to school. I wanted to tell him to take a breath."

"You didn't, did you?" Phyllis asked.

"Oh, no. Anyway, as smart as he is, it was pretty good conversation. Funny, too." Sam poured himself some coffee and went on, "What's on the agenda for the rest of the day?"

"I'm not sure. I thought about talking to Brian Flynn again. But if I come right out and tell him I know he used to date Roxanne in high school . . ."

"He's liable to clam up and not say anything else."

Phyllis nodded. "I'm afraid so. I'd also like to know if he ever came around the beauty salon while Roxanne was working there."

"Times when Danny wasn't around, you mean?"

"Exactly."

Carolyn said, "If they were having an affair, they wouldn't meet where Roxanne worked. That would have been too blatant."

"And they couldn't very well get together at the paint and body shop," Sam said. "Roxanne wouldn't have had any excuse for bein' there when Danny wasn't."

Phyllis considered all that and nodded. "So they met elsewhere. The farm house, maybe? Brian could have told Danny he was going to go pick up some parts or something whenever he had a rendezvous with Roxanne."

"Or maybe wherever Brian lives," Sam said. "To tell you the truth, I never did any sneakin' around like that, so I don't really know how it works."

"Neither did I," Phyllis said.

Carolyn turned her head and gave Eve a long, speculative look.

"What are you looking at me for?" Eve demanded. "*I* never played around with a married man!"

"Really?" Carolyn said.

"Yes, really! Why do you think I got married so many times? If they wanted it, they had to put a ring on it. I'm no more an expert on adultery than any of the rest of you."

"All right," Phyllis said. "Let's start with Estelle Prentice, Sam. You remember her."

"The lady who keeps her horses in the field across the road from the Jackson place?"

"That's right. She said she lives in White Settlement. Let's see if we can find an address for her."

Looking up someone's address and phone number online was fairly easy if you didn't mind paying for the service. Phyllis had found in previous cases that the expense was well worth it. Jimmy D'Angelo would usually reimburse her for things like that, but she didn't even make a note of it this time.

This was Danny, Mike's old friend, and her efforts were strictly *pro bono.* She couldn't make any money off someone who had sat at her kitchen table eating peanut butter and jelly sandwiches.

There were a number of people named Prentice who lived in White Settlement, but only one with the initials E.F. Phyllis recalled that Estelle had said her husband had passed away, so it was possible the phone was in her name. The fact that it was a landline was another indication that its owner was an older person, since a lot of young people had done away with what they considered an antiquated system.

"Are you gonna give her a call?" Sam asked when Phyllis had found the name and address on the computer.

"No, I don't think so. Maybe we can catch her at home. I'd like to talk to her face to face."

"That'll probably mean droppin' the story about paintin' old farm houses."

"That's fine," Phyllis said. "I think it's

probably time we started dropping some pretenses."

She put the address she believed belonged to Estelle Prentice into her phone, then she and Sam set out. White Settlement was on the west side of Fort Worth and had been there since pioneer days, but it had only begun to flourish during the Second World War, when it served as a bedroom community for the nearby Consolidated-Vultee aircraft plant where the B-24 Liberator bomber had been manufactured. The so-called "bomber plant" was still there, although it had gone through numerous name and ownership changes and had turned out many different types of aircraft over the years, but many of the people who worked there still lived in White Settlement. A lot of other businesses had moved in, too, and it was now a bustling suburban city.

Many of the residential streets still looked the same as they had fifty or sixty years earlier, however, including the one Phyllis and Sam found themselves driving down half an hour after leaving Weatherford. It was lined with frame, one-story houses, most of them appearing to be well cared for behind neat lawns and flower beds.

"If it weren't for the cars parked along here, it'd be almost like we were back in

1957," Sam commented. "In some ways, that wouldn't be a bad thing."

"But in some it would," Phyllis said. "There have been a lot of advances in society and technology since then."

"That's true. It's a shame we can't sorta take the best of both worlds and leave the bad parts behind."

Phyllis couldn't argue with that.

She pointed out the street number they were looking for. It was painted on a mailbox next to the driveway of a light green house with white metal awnings extending over the windows. Shrubs grew along the front of the house, next to the small front porch. There was an attached one-car garage and a pickup parked in the driveway. Phyllis thought she recognized it from their encounter with Estelle Prentice a few days earlier.

"This must be it," she said.

"And it looks like she's home," Sam replied. He parked his pickup at the curb, and they got out.

Phyllis pushed the doorbell next to the screen door. A moment later the wooden inside door opened and Estelle Prentice looked out. She said, "Can I help — Wait a minute. I recognize the two of you." She nodded toward Sam. "Especially you,

207

Stretch. What can I do for you? I know you're not here to make a painting out of my house!"

"I'm afraid we fibbed a little bit to you the other day, Mrs. Prentice," Phyllis began.

"So you *are* real estate people. I don't care if you want to buy my property out there on Silver Creek Road. It's not for sale. The scavengers can come along and fight over it when I'm dead and gone."

Sam held up a hand and said, "We're not realtors, and we're not lookin' to buy any property."

"We're investigating Roxanne Jackson's murder," Phyllis said.

Estelle's eyebrows went up in surprise. "You're detectives? A couple of old geezers like you?"

Sam grinned and said, "Right on both counts."

"Really?"

"It's true," Phyllis said. "We're working for the attorney handling Danny Jackson's appeal."

"You mean you're trying to get him off after he killed that poor girl?" Estelle reached for the door as if she intended to slam it.

"We don't believe he's guilty," Phyllis said quickly. "We're not just investigators. I've

208

known Danny since he was a little boy. He was my son's best friend in school. Regardless of how the case looks, I know he couldn't have killed Roxanne."

Estelle squinted suspiciously at them for several seconds, then said, "Well, why didn't you say so to start with? What are you doing here? You got questions for me?"

"That's right."

"Well, come on in," Estelle said, still with obvious reluctance. "I suppose it wouldn't hurt anything to talk to you for a few minutes."

She let them into a living room that looked very much like the one in Phyllis's house, not surprising since they were from the same generation and same general background. Phyllis and Sam sat on a sofa with crocheted doilies draped over the tops of the cushions. Estelle sat in an armchair opposite them, next to a big TV in a heavy wooden cabinet that had to be at least forty years old.

"What do you want to know?"

Phyllis had saved and printed out two pictures from Facebook: the one of Danny and Brian when they opened their shop and the yearbook picture of Brian and Roxanne. She took them from her purse and stood up to hand them across to Estelle.

"Could you look at them and tell us if you've ever seen that blond man?"

Estelle took the pictures and studied them. A couple of minutes went by before she said, "This is the same guy in the yearbook picture and the later picture, isn't it?"

"That's right."

"He was Roxanne's boyfriend in high school?"

"Yes."

"And Danny's friend now."

"They're business partners," Phyllis said.

Estelle looked up. "Does Danny know about this guy and Roxanne?"

Phyllis shook her head and said, "We don't think so." Eventually they were going to have to confirm that with Danny, she told herself. She had hoped to postpone that until they had more answers, just to avoid upsetting Danny unnecessarily, but that might not be possible.

"You ever see that fella out at the farm house across from your pasture?" Sam asked.

"Especially if he was with Roxanne when Danny wasn't around," Phyllis added.

"Oh, I get it," Estelle said. "You think there was some hanky-panky goin' on."

"It's possible. High school sweethearts

getting back together again . . ." Phyllis's voice trailed off as Estelle began shaking her head.

"I hate to disappoint you, but I never saw this guy before in my life." She poked at one of the pictures with a fingernail, and Phyllis knew she was indicating Brian Flynn. "I can't say he was never there, mind you. But *I* never saw him."

"We're not disappointed," Phyllis said. "We just wanted to know what information you might have, and you told us."

"Roxanne never confided anything about her personal life to you, did she?" Sam asked.

"You mean like telling me she was havin' an affair?" Estelle let out a curt bark of laughter. "Not hardly. We were friendly acquaintances, that's all. It's not like she would spill her guts to me."

That comment made Phyllis frown in thought as something tickled the back of her mind again, but she couldn't identify it.

"Look, I wish I could help you," Estelle went on. "I was friendlier with Roxanne than I was with Danny, but I don't have anything against the kid. If he didn't do it, he shouldn't go to prison for it."

"That's the way we feel," Phyllis said. "Thank you for talking to us."

211

"Sure." The woman cocked her head to the side. "So you don't paint pictures of farm houses after all, eh?"

"I have no artistic ability whatsoever," Phyllis said. "Being able to paint is like . . . magic to me."

"But she can solve murders," Sam said. "That's an art."

Phyllis was starting to be not so sure about that.

CHAPTER 19

"Where to now?" Sam asked as they got back into the pickup a few minutes later.

"Why don't you drive by the paint and body shop?" Phyllis said. "I want to talk to Brian again, if I can do it without spooking him."

"If he didn't do anything, there won't be any reason for him to spook."

"Maybe not, but I intend to be careful anyway."

It took about ten minutes to reach the stretch of Highway 377 where Lone Star Paint and Body was located. As they approached the business, Phyllis said, "Slow down. Brian's out front talking to someone."

"I'll pull in here at this convenience store," Sam said as he turned the wheel and steered the pickup smoothly into the store's parking lot. There was nothing about the move to draw any attention. "Can you still see the place from here?"

"Yes, but I'm not sure there's any real reason for us to be skulking around like this. He's probably just talking to a customer."

The conversation was taking place in front of one of the open repair bays. An expensive SUV was parked in front of the office. Brian, wearing his usual coveralls, was talking to a woman with long blond hair. He moved back a little, just inside the bay, and the woman went with him. Phyllis could still see both of them, although they were in the shadows now and not as clear.

Clear enough, though, for her to see Brian take the woman into his arms and kiss her.

"Well," Sam said, "probably not a customer after all, unless Brian's runnin' a special deal on, uh, body work."

"I wouldn't be at all surprised if he carries on with some of his customers," Phyllis said. "A young man as good-looking as he is probably has plenty of opportunities. He told us he doesn't intend to settle down any time soon."

Inside the repair bay, the kiss continued for a long moment. The woman, whose hair fell halfway down her back, had her arms around Brian's neck and her body plastered to his. Eventually, though, they moved apart. They exchanged a few more words, then the woman walked to the car in front of the office, climbed in, and drove away. Phyllis had gotten a good enough look at her to know she was attractive, but that was all.

"You still want to go talk to him?" Sam asked.

Phyllis thought about it, then nodded and said, "Yes. Just because one of his girlfriends stopped by his shop doesn't change anything."

Sam parked the pickup in front of the office. Brian came out of the repair bays, wiping his hands on a rag. He smiled at them and said, "Mrs. Newsom, Mr. Fletcher, good to see you again. Have you got news about Danny? You're gonna get him back here pretty soon so he can help me out with all this work, right?"

"I still hope so," Phyllis said, "but we don't have any news, just a few more questions."

"Sure. Come on in the shop, out of the sun." Brian grinned. "If you don't tell the insurance company, I won't."

He leaned against a car with a crumpled front fender and crossed his arms, waiting to hear what Phyllis had to say.

"Do you remember Danny mentioning anything about Roxanne getting in trouble at the beauty salon?" she asked. "About a customer who was so upset they were talking about a lawsuit?"

"A lawsuit?" Brian repeated. "Over a haircut or a facial? That's crazy!"

"Some people's appearance is very important to them."

"Yeah, but hair will grow back." Brian shook his head. "No, I don't recall Danny saying anything about that. He didn't talk much about the salon. I don't think Roxanne told him a lot about what went on there." He shrugged. "And Danny wouldn't care about a lot of gossip, anyway. No offense, but isn't that what women do in places like that? Just gossip and talk trash about their friends?"

"Sometimes," Phyllis said. "Were you ever with Danny when he stopped at the salon?"

"Once or twice, I think. Sometimes we'd go get something to eat, then stop by there if he needed to talk to Roxanne. But like I said, that only happened a couple of times, at most."

"Do you know any of the other people who work there? The lady who owns the salon, maybe, or the receptionist? Aurora is her name, I believe."

Brian thought about it, then slowly shook his head. "No, not really. I kinda remember the girl who works up at the front. Always has her hair dyed some funny color."

"That's her," Phyllis said.

"I guess I'm an old-fashioned guy in some ways. I like for a woman's hair to be its natural color, or at least a color you can find in nature. Never cared much for all the blue and pink and green hair, things like that."

"Got to say I agree with you about that," Sam put in.

Brian looked more serious as he said, "Do you think Roxanne's murder was caused by something that happened at the salon?"

"We're still just trying to consider all the possibilities," Phyllis said.

"That doesn't sound too promising."

"So far it's not. But we're not going to give up. We'll keep digging until we get to the truth."

"For Danny's sake, I'm glad to hear that. If there's anything I can do . . ."

"We'll let you know," Phyllis promised.

As they drove away a few minutes later, Sam said, "Well, I don't reckon we know any more than we did."

Phyllis didn't say anything, but her forehead was creased in a frown when she didn't respond and Sam looked over at her.

"You've figured it out," he said, excitement coming into his voice.

"No," she said, "I haven't. But I've seen or heard something that's important. I can tell that. Let's go to the salon."

If anyone had pressed her, Phyllis wouldn't have been able to say why she told Sam to head for Paul's Beauty Salon. It was instinct, a sense that a connection existed she hadn't made consciously, but something in her brain was trying to tell her what it was. She hoped that by following her hunch, everything would become clear . . . or at least less obscure.

Along the way, she took out the copy of the yearbook picture she had printed and studied it intently. The other times she had looked at it, her attention had been focused on Brian and Roxanne. Now she looked at the other four young people and checked their names in the caption. The handsome football players were Derek Nelson and Nathan Morgan. The pretty cheerleaders, a blonde and a brunette, were D.J. Hutton and Kirsten Gregory. None of those names meant a thing to Phyllis, and she didn't recognize any of them.

"You got a mighty serious look on your face," Sam said. "Hate to interrupt you, but we're almost there."

Phyllis looked up from the photograph

and sighed. "I'm not doing any good anyway. I'm trying to cudgel my brain into working, but it doesn't want to cooperate."

"Cudgel," Sam repeated. "That's a word I haven't heard in a long time. It's a good one, though. Sometimes it really fits. Like bludgeon."

"That reminds me too much of what happened to Roxanne. On the other hand, reminders are good, because they help keep me focused on helping Danny." Phyllis looked over at him. "Do you remember how many times Roxanne was hit, according to the medical examiner's testimony at the trial?"

"I couldn't tell you for sure," Sam said as he pulled into the parking lot in front of the salon. "Quite a few, though. A couple dozen? Enough to make it a really ugly murder. Is that important?"

"It tells us the killer was angry."

"Well, he'd have to be pretty mad to —"

"Not necessarily. A killer can strike with cold deliberation. If all he wanted was for Roxanne to die, a few blows might have been enough to accomplish that. The way he kept on hitting her again and again tells me he had a lot of rage directed toward her bottled up inside him."

"Which takes us back to Brian or Danny,

the two fellas we know were involved with her romantically. You know the old sayin' about there bein' a thin line between love and hate."

"You don't have to be in a relationship to feel rage toward another person."

"No, but if somebody snaps, passion — one way or the other — could sure fuel what comes next."

Phyllis nodded. Everything Sam said was true, but it didn't seem to fit with the vague picture forming in her mind. She tried to force it, and it just wouldn't go.

She put that aside for the moment and opened the pickup door.

"You don't have to come in with me," she told Sam.

He opened his door as well. "When you're on the trail of a killer like this, you're not goin' anywhere without me," he said.

They walked into the salon, which was busy as usual. Aurora was the only one in the reception area, however. She looked surprised to see them and said, "Hello. I don't think your mani/pedi appointment is until next week, Mrs. Newsom, but I can check . . ."

"No need to check," Phyllis said. "I'm not here for that. I'd like to ask you a question, if you don't mind."

"Sure," Aurora said with a slight shrug.

Phyllis took one of the pictures from her purse and set it on the desk. "I know you probably recognize Danny Jackson, but do you know the man in this picture with him?"

Aurora frowned as she looked at the photograph Phyllis had printed, then raised her head.

"What is this?" she asked. "I remember you talked some about Roxanne before, and so did you, Mr. Fletcher. What's going on here? What business is it of yours who I know?"

"You're not in any trouble —" Sam began.

"I'm not so sure about that." Aurora pushed her chair back a little, as if trying to put some distance between her and the two of them, but not so far that she couldn't reach the phone. She picked it up, pushed a button on it, and said, "Pauline, could you come out here right now?" Her tone of voice showed how spooked she was. She paused for a second and then said, "Please." She hung up the phone and said to Phyllis and Sam, "You should talk to my aunt."

"We're really not trying to cause a problem," Phyllis said. "We just need a little information."

"What are you? Cops?" Aurora shook her head. "I don't think so. Not at your age."

"We're not police," Phyllis said, "but we are investigators —"

Pauline opened one of the glass doors, stepped into the reception area, and said in a clearly annoyed tone, "What is this?"

"These two showed up and started asking questions about Roxanne and her husband again," Aurora told her aunt. "It was kind of weird before, but now it's starting to get crazy. They claim to be detectives of some sort."

"Aurora, now take it easy," Pauline said, her voice dulcet and soothing again. "I'm sure Phyllis and . . . ?" She looked at Sam.

He supplied his name. "Sam Fletcher, Miz Gibbs. And just so you'll know, Phyllis and I aren't delusional."

"I never said you were."

"And we didn't ask about Roxanne and Danny," Phyllis said. She tapped a finger on the photograph that still lay on the desk. "We asked about this man."

Pauline had the same instinctive reaction as Aurora. She looked down at the picture and said, "That's Roxanne's husband, but I'm not sure about the other man — Wait. That's the man who owns that garage with him, isn't it?"

"It's a paint and body shop," Aurora said. Phyllis thought she had probably spent more time talking to Danny than Pauline had. "And yes, that's him. I don't remember his name. Brad? Something like that?"

Phyllis and Sam looked at each other. Phyllis's instincts told her that Aurora was telling the truth, and Sam's tiny nod showed that he agreed with her.

"I'll be honest with you," she said to Pauline and Aurora.

Pauline folded her arms across her chest and said, "That might be nice for a change."

"Like I told Aurora, we're investigators. We work for the lawyer who's handling Danny Jackson's appeal. We're trying to find proof that he didn't kill Roxanne."

"Who else could have?"

"That's what we're trying to figure out. But we think this man might have had something to do with it." Phyllis pointed again to the photo of Brian Flynn.

"Y'all already know who he is. It's not like you need us to identify him."

"What we needed was confirmation that he'd been here at the salon."

"He was here," Pauline said. "Once or twice with Roxanne's husband, anyway."

"But that's all? He never came around when Danny wasn't with him?"

"Not that I remember." Pauline looked at Aurora. "How about you?"

"No, it's like you said, Pauline. He was with Danny a couple of times. I remember him because . . . Well, look at him. He's gorgeous."

Phyllis wouldn't have gone that far, but she wasn't 25 years old anymore, either.

"Did he talk to anybody?" she asked.

"Here at the salon?" Aurora shook her head. "No, he just came in with Danny, and they both waited out here while Roxanne stepped out so Danny could talk to her. I don't remember what it was about, but I don't think it was anything important."

"Did Brian talk to you while he was here? That's his name, Brian Flynn."

Aurora made a scoffing sound and said, "Hell, no. He was too busy looking in there." She nodded toward the glass doors. "Something was sure fascinating to him. He acted like he'd never seen the inside of a beauty shop before." She grimaced and added hastily, "Beauty salon. Sorry, Pauline."

"You're sure about all that?" Phyllis said.

"I just told you, didn't I? That's what happened. Now that you've reminded me of it, I remember it pretty clearly."

Aurora picked up the photograph and looked at it again.

"Is he a killer?" she asked.

"Brian? We don't know yet."

"It would sure be a shame if he was. Somebody who looks like that, I mean."

She handed the photograph to Phyllis, who put it back in her purse.

Pauline squinted at them in suspicion and anger and said, "So when you were here before, you came under false pretenses. You were just looking for information for this . . . this case you're working on."

"That's true, I suppose," Phyllis admitted. "But Courtney and Talia did a really, really good job on my hair and face."

"I'll second that," Sam put in.

Pauline shrugged and said, "A customer's a customer, I guess, no matter what brings 'em in. I don't appreciate bein' lied to, though. You could've told us who you really are and asked your questions."

"No, they couldn't have!" Aurora exclaimed. "I just figured it out. They thought somebody here at the salon killed Roxanne! Maybe you or me!"

"Good Lord," Pauline muttered. "Is that true?"

"We hadn't ruled out anybody at that time," Phyllis said. In truth, they hadn't ruled out the possibility now, but it was looking more unlikely all the time.

"None of us would have hurt Roxanne,"

Pauline declared flatly. "She was one of the best stylists I ever had here."

"She nearly got you sued," Phyllis said.

"Only because Shelley Dawson is a crazy bitch! I know I shouldn't say that about somebody who's in a wheelchair, but shoot, bein' in a wheelchair doesn't mean you're all sweetness and light. I was upset with Roxanne for a while, but that would have blown over without any problem." Pauline hesitated, frowning. "What really bothered me was how Roxanne just didn't seem to care anymore. The job she did on Shelley Dawson *wasn't* her best work. The way she was actin', I expected her to give me her notice any day. She sure changed."

Pauline wasn't the only one who had mentioned that change in Roxanne's attitude. Was it connected with whatever had gotten her killed? Phyllis had to think there was a good chance it was.

"All right," she said. "We appreciate you talking to us. You didn't have to."

"To be honest, I thought about tellin' you to take a hike," Pauline said. "But I guess you're just tryin' to do your jobs."

"We don't want an innocent man going to prison for a murder he didn't commit."

"Neither do I. I sure thought it was an open-and-shut case against Roxanne's

226

husband, though."

"The killer was probably counting on everybody thinking that," Phyllis said.

CHAPTER 20

"You figure they were tellin' the truth?" Sam asked as they drove away a short time later.

"About Brian only being there a couple of times, and only with Danny?" Phyllis thought about it for a second before nodding. "I think so. Aurora seemed genuinely offended by the fact that Brian didn't pay any attention to her."

"Well, Roxanne was there."

"But he wasn't looking at her," Phyllis pointed out. "He was looking into the salon, Aurora said. And Roxanne was out in the reception area talking to Danny at the time."

"Yeah, you're right. So, what was he so interested in?"

"I don't know yet," Phyllis said.

"Had to be one of the other stylists, or maybe a customer," Sam said. "There's nothin' fascinatin' about a hair dryer or a sink."

"No, there's not."

"Too bad we can't find out who-all was there that day."

Phyllis reached into her purse and took out one of the photographs. She looked at it for a few seconds, then said, "Maybe we won't have to. Let's head for home. I need to do some more research."

The nebulous thoughts in her head were starting to form a picture, but there were still some large blank spots in it. She could speculate about what might fit in them, but that was all it would be, pure speculation.

Phyllis was silent for the most part on the drive back to Weatherford. When they got home, it was nearly time for Sam to go pick up Bobby at school. He headed for the backyard to get Buck, so he could take the Dalmatian with him. There were few things Buck liked better than riding in the pickup. He was fairly well behaved about it, too, spending most of his time looking out the window.

After saying a rather distracted hello to Carolyn and Eve, Phyllis went to the computer and began searching for four names: Derek Nelson, Nathan Morgan, D.J. Hutton, and Kirsten Gregory.

She drew a blank on the two girls. They were probably married by now — they could have been married two or three times, the way people discarded spouses these days — and she had no idea what their last names currently were.

She found an obituary for Nathan Morgan, killed in Iraq by an IED. His date of birth, plus the fact that he had gone to Western Hills High School, told Phyllis she had found the tall, lanky, dark-haired football player in the yearbook photo. She had the printed picture lying on the desk, and she couldn't help but look at his grinning, youthful face and think about how his life had been cut tragically short. But so had Roxanne's.

The only one she had any luck with was Derek Nelson. She found Facebook and LinkedIn pages for him and discovered that he worked for a financial management firm in Fort Worth. A glance at the time told her it was still business hours, but it was also Friday afternoon, so there was a chance Derek Nelson might have left the office early.

There was only one way to find out, Phyllis thought as she took out her cell phone and called Nelson's firm.

Nelson answered his own phone, which was a little surprising. Phyllis introduced herself, then said, "If you've got a minute,

I'd really like to ask you a couple of questions."

"You don't have an Indian accent, so I haven't hung up on you yet, Mrs. . . . Newsom, was it? But I really don't have time for one those phony surveys —"

"This isn't a survey, Mr. Nelson, I promise you that. I work for an attorney named Jimmy D'Angelo over in Weatherford, and I'm doing some research on a murder case. I think you can help me."

For a moment, there was silence on the other end of the connection. Then Nelson said, "Is this for real? Are you pulling some sort of prank, lady?"

"Not at all. You can look up Mr. D'Angelo's number, call his office, and ask them about me if you'd like. I'd be glad to give you time to do that, then call you back."

"No, no, you certainly *sound* believable. And you've got me curious. Just what is it you want?"

"Do you remember going to high school with a man named Brian Flynn?"

"Brian? Sure. We played ball together." Nelson's voice sharpened as he went on, "Something hasn't happened to him, has it? You said this was about a murder —"

"No, Mr. Flynn's fine, as far as I know."

"Well, I'm glad to hear that. I haven't seen

him or talked to him in . . . oh, ten years or more. Are you looking for him?"

"No, he has a business in Fort Worth. I've spoken with him a couple of times in the past week."

"Okay. Then I don't see how me remembering him does you any good, if you already know where he is."

"What about his girlfriend, Roxanne Macrae?"

Nelson laughed. "You mean one of his girlfriends. Brian was never the sort to confine himself to one girl for very long. Oh, he was faithful enough while he was dating somebody, I guess, but he went through them pretty quick."

"That must have caused some hard feelings," Phyllis said.

"Sure, but not toward Brian. He had the knack, you know. Trouble just sort of slid off him. The girls would blame each other, not him. The rest of the guys on the team never could figure out how he did it." Nelson paused, and when he went on, it was in a reminiscing tone. "I'm trying to remember the girl Brian dated before Roxanne. She wasn't too happy when Brian dumped her for one of the other cheerleaders."

Phyllis took a shot. "Was it Kirsten Gregory?"

"What? No. Kirsten was my girlfriend for more than a year. She never dated Brian, that I recall."

"What about D.J. Hutton?"

"That's who it was!" Nelson laughed again. "Brian dumped her for Roxanne, and she wound up dating Nate Morgan. That worked out good for Nate. He never was what you'd call suave, so getting a girl like D.J., even if it was because Brian didn't want her anymore, was a break for him."

"Do you know where she is now?"

"D.J.? I have no idea. I've tried to keep up with the people in my class, you know. It's, well, it's good business. But some of them I've lost track of, like Brian. D.J.'s another one. And Nate . . ." Nelson's voice turned solemn. "Oh, man, Nate, poor guy. Went to Iraq but didn't make it out alive."

"I'm sorry," Phyllis said, even though she already knew that about Nathan Morgan.

"I'd still like to know what this is all about, Mrs. Newsom."

"It's a long story, but basically, Roxanne Macrae was murdered, and I'm trying to help find out who killed her."

A couple of seconds of silence went by, then Nelson said, "Damn. I'm sorry to hear that. I was never really close to Roxanne back in high school, but she was a sweet kid. Got along all right with everybody, as far as I remember. As long as they didn't cross her."

Phyllis's grip on the phone tightened. She asked, "What do you mean by that, Mr. Nelson?"

"Well, like I said, she was sweet, but when she wanted something, she had a tendency to really go after it, you know what I mean? Like being the captain of the cheerleaders. And Brian, too. She wanted him, she went after him, and she got him. Didn't do her any good in the long run, nobody could ever tie that guy down, not even Roxie. But she tried."

That matched what Phyllis knew about Roxanne: smart, a hard worker, and ambitious . . . until suddenly she wasn't. That was still perplexing.

"Was there anything else?" Nelson asked. The question broke into Phyllis's thoughts.

"No, that's all," she said. "You've been very helpful."

"I hope so. And I hope you find out who killed Roxie. Too many of the people I went to school with are gone already, and I'm not even forty yet! It's enough to make you think about the future. Do you have your future lined up, Mrs. Newsom, especially the financial aspects of it?"

Over the phone like this, he couldn't tell that he was talking to a woman of fairly advanced age, Phyllis thought. Her voice didn't really show it. And she didn't want to listen to his pitch, so she said, "Yes, I do. Thank you again," and broke the connection before he could go on.

The picture was almost there now, she thought, but it was still missing a few pieces. Her gut told her that when she uncovered them, she would have a pretty good idea of who had really killed Roxanne Jackson, and why.

So for now, all she could do was keep looking.

Sam came in with Bobby a few minutes later, and with that Phyllis had to put the investigation on hold for the time being. Her grandson needed her attention, and family came first.

Also, Eve had talked to her friend who grew berries, and there were still some blackberries available to be picked. With the next day being Saturday, Phyllis knew Bobby would need something to do, so an expedition to the berry farm might be just the thing.

Besides, she had reached the point where everything she had learned about Roxanne Jackson's life and death needed to percolate for a while in her brain. Once it did, she believed things would be clearer.

The heat wave of earlier in the week, which had coincided with the air conditioner problems, had broken, and the air was cooler, dryer, and more comfortable the next day as all five of them set out for the farm. Sam had mentioned taking Buck along as well, but Carolyn had quickly and effectively shot down that idea.

"Turn a dog loose in a field full of bushes, and what do you think he's going to do?" she had asked.

"Oh, yeah, that's probably right," Sam said, then shrugged and added, "Well, it was just an idea."

"Not a very good one."

They all wore jeans, long-sleeved shirts, and straw hats to protect themselves from the sun. As they walked out into the long, wide field full of plants, Eve said, "I look rustically adorable, don't I?"

"There aren't any of your Hollywood producer friends here to see you," Carolyn said, "so I wouldn't worry about it too much."

"A lady should always worry about how

she looks," Eve replied. "I mean, Phyllis is positively glamorous since her trip to that salon."

Phyllis made a dismissive sound and said, "Let's not get carried away."

"That's right," Sam said. "You were glamorous before you ever went there."

"I've never seen the appeal of salons and spas and things like that," Carolyn said. "Having your hair done is fine, but all those other things . . . getting massages and having goop smeared on your face and waxing . . . it's just a waste of time."

Phyllis was watching Bobby run ahead in the field and didn't pay much attention to what Carolyn was saying, but she replied, "Paul's is a salon, not a spa. I don't think they do massages or waxing. But I didn't ask, so I don't know for sure."

"Well, people are too concerned about appearances, that's all I'm saying."

"You can never be too concerned about your appearance," Eve argued. "If you don't care anymore, then what's the point of going on?"

"You care about other things," Carolyn said.

"You and I are just separated by an unimaginable gulf of opinion, dear."

"Did we come to pick berries or talk?"

Phyllis hefted the straw bushel basket Eve's friend had provided. Each of them had one. "We're here to pick berries," she said. "I have a pie to make, after all."

Sam called, "Don't eat too many of 'em, Bobby. Your stomach won't thank you later."

"And those berries haven't even been washed!" Phyllis exclaimed as she hurried toward her grandson. "There's no telling what might be on them."

Bobby looked up at her, his already berry-stained lips stretched in a grin, and she knew she was probably fighting a losing battle.

CHAPTER 21

After church the next morning and Sunday dinner of slow cook honey sesame chicken served on rice, Phyllis spent part of the afternoon preparing her black and blueberry pie and getting it in the oven to bake. Her mother never would have done that, she reflected. A devoutly religious Southern Baptist, Phyllis's mother would have considered that work, and you weren't supposed to work on the Sabbath. Preparing dinner didn't count, because of course you had to feed your family regardless of what day of the week it was. Phyllis didn't consider baking to be work, though, so she didn't think there was anything particularly sinful about popping a pie into the oven.

"That's done," she said as she came into the living room. Eve wasn't there, so Phyllis supposed she was upstairs in her room, possibly working on her next book. Carolyn sat in a comfortable chair by the window, her knitting in her lap as the pair of needles worked adroitly in her fingers. Bobby was at the computer while Sam sat beside him, phone in hand.

"What are you two doing?" Phyllis asked them.

"Playin' World of Warcraft," Sam said. "Bobby just chopped off an ogre's head with his battle ax."

Phyllis drew in a deep breath and leaned forward. "What?"

Bobby turned his head to look up at her and pointed at the screen. "I just caught a fish!" he said.

"It's a bass fishin' game," Sam said with a grin. "I'm sorry. The look on your face was worth it, though."

"And what are *you* doing?" Phyllis asked ominously.

"Me? I'm playin' World of Warcraft."

"No, you're not."

He turned the screen around so she could see it.

"Well, maybe you are," Phyllis said. "I wouldn't know. Anyway, there are too many monsters in real life to spend your time fighting make-believe ones."

"Yeah . . . but sometimes you can beat the make-believe ones."

Phyllis wasn't sure what to say to that, so

she just left Sam and Bobby to their games and sat down on the sofa to read the newspaper. Not many people had the actual print edition delivered anymore, but she still subscribed to the Sunday paper even though, like a lot of things in this modern world, it was a mere shadow of what it had once been. She didn't like the idea of getting *all* her news from the Internet.

Besides, there was something comforting about sitting back, putting your feet up, setting the paper in your lap, and then going through it section by section, reading the whole thing from front to back. She remembered her father doing that every Sunday afternoon for years and years. Church, dinner, the newspaper, and then a baseball game on TV, if one was on. Late in the afternoon, there was a locally broadcast program of gospel music, and her father would whistle along beautifully . . .

Phyllis felt a pang inside for those by-gone days. More and more lately, her thoughts had been turning back, back, to simpler times, and the waves of melancholy that washed over at those moments could be almost overwhelming.

She swallowed hard. Better to concentrate on the here and now, she told herself. She opened the newspaper . . .

And the first words to catch her eye were *Attempted Murder.*

She almost didn't read the story, thinking that she didn't need any more ugliness to occupy her thoughts right now. Something drew her on, though, so she continued reading. According to the story, someone had broken into the home of wealthy Fort Worth businessman Hugh Chilton on Saturday night and shot both Chilton and his wife Desiree. Mrs. Chilton's wounds were not life-threatening, but her husband was in critical condition and not expected to survive. According to a police department spokesman, Hugh Chilton had probably saved his wife's life because he had managed to get his hands on a pistol he owned and had fired a shot at the gunman, striking him and forcing him to flee, before succumbing to his own injuries. The apparent motive for the attack had been robbery. Mrs. Chilton was still hospitalized but was expected to be released soon.

Phyllis didn't realize how long she had been sitting there unmoving, staring at the newspaper, until Carolyn said, "Phyllis? Are you all right?"

Phyllis gave a little start, lowered the paper, and said, "Yes, I'm fine. I must have dozed off a little."

"Yeah, it's gettin' to be that time of day," Sam said. "Might try to get a nap myself, once I get done battlin' these orcs. How's the fishin' comin' along, Bobby?"

"I've caught a bunch of 'em!" the little boy said.

Phyllis turned the page. The pie was starting to smell good. They would sample it later, after it came out of the oven and had a chance to cool a little. The lazy Sunday would continue. For a change, no one had asked her if she had just solved Roxanne Jackson's murder.

But she had.

The black and blueberry pie, everyone agreed, was delicious. Sweet enough without being too sweet, and bursting with fresh fruit flavor from the blackberries they had picked the day before mixed with some nice blueberries she'd found at a farmer's market.. A scoop of vanilla ice cream on it led Bobby to proclaim it the best thing he had ever eaten.

"You probably shouldn't mention that around your mother," Phyllis told him, "but I do appreciate it."

A little later, Mike called from California with good news. The doctors had determined that Sarah's mother had suffered a mild heart attack, but she was in stable condition and no real danger.

"Sarah's going to be staying out here for a while, but I'll fly back Tuesday," Mike went on.

"Stay as long as you need to," Phyllis told him. "We're taking good care of Bobby, and I think he's having a fine time."

"You don't know how much it means to us that we can depend on you like this, Mom."

"I'm happy to have him here," Phyllis said.

"What about Danny's case?"

Phyllis hesitated. She didn't want to get his hopes up in case her theory turned out to be completely wrong. She didn't think it would, but there was still a matter of proof.

"Maybe I'll have some news by the time you get back," she said.

"I hope so. That would wrap things up nicely."

Wouldn't it, though, Phyllis thought.

There was no more talk of murder in the house that evening. Everyone seemed to have forgotten about the case . . . which was just the way Phyllis wanted it for now.

She didn't tell Sam that she had figured it out until after he got back from taking Bobby to school Monday morning.

"You mean you know who killed Roxanne?" he asked her, his shaggy eyebrows lifting in surprise.

"I have a pretty good idea. I can see almost the entire thing now. I just need to clarify one more point." She sighed. "And it's something I should have asked about a long time ago. The key was right there from the start, but I just didn't see it."

"You gonna tell me what it is?"

"I want to wait until I'm absolutely sure," she said. "And I'll have to explain everything to Mr. D'Angelo, too, so maybe it would be better just to cover everything at once."

"So what's our next move?"

"We're going to jail," Phyllis said.

She called D'Angelo's office and asked him if he could get her in to see Danny.

"The sooner the better," she added.

"Holy Toledo!" the lawyer exclaimed. "You've figured it out!"

Ah, there it was. Phyllis smiled slightly as she said, "I think so. I need to talk to Danny, though."

"I'll call you just as soon as I've got it set up."

By now Carolyn and Eve had figured out what was going on. Eve said, "I *knew* I could count on you, dear. You never let me down."

"She wasn't doing it for you," Carolyn said. "She was trying to help Danny Jackson. The only way it has any connection with you is it might generate more interest in your book."

"And the sequels," Eve said.

"You mean you're doing *more* of them?"

"Why not, as long as people like to read them?"

Carolyn walked off, muttering about how she would never understand it.

Phyllis's cell phone rang. It was Jimmy D'Angelo, and the lawyer said, "How soon can you be ready to go?"

"Right away," Phyllis told him.

"Good. I'll swing by there in a few minutes and pick up you and Sam. We can take my car."

Phyllis had assumed she and Sam would drive over to Fort Worth in his pickup, but if D'Angelo wanted to pick them up, she supposed that was all right.

"We'll be ready," she said.

D'Angelo pulled up at the curb a few minutes later in a big black Cadillac. "Looks like a gangster's car," Sam said quietly to Phyllis as they went out the walk toward the Caddy. "I always figured Jimmy must'a been mobbed up at one time. That's probably why he left the East Coast."

"You have a very vivid imagination, don't you?"

"Sometimes." Sam grinned. "But sometimes I'm right, too. And hey, everybody's got secrets. Maybe we'll find out Jimmy's, one of these days."

They got in the car, Phyllis in front, Sam in the back so he could stretch his long legs across the floorboard.

"All right, spill," D'Angelo said as he pulled away from the curb.

"After I've talked to Danny," Phyllis replied.

"She wouldn't tell me, either," Sam put in. "Sometimes she'll talk about what she's thinkin', and sometimes she won't explain until she's got the whole thing nailed down."

D'Angelo said, "I'm highly skilled at cross-examination, you know."

"Doesn't matter. If Phyllis doesn't want to talk, you won't get a thing out of her."

D'Angelo sighed. "Well, then, I suppose I'll have to be patient."

"Honestly," Phyllis said, "you're both making me feel like I'm being mean. I just want to make sure I have everything straight in my head so I won't waste everyone's time with something crazy."

The big Cadillac was fast and nearly silent. D'Angelo didn't waste any time getting to Fort Worth. It took a while to navigate the red tape of getting in to see Danny, though, once they reached the jail.

Finally, Phyllis and D'Angelo were sitting across from him in one of the spartanly furnished visitors' rooms. The bruises and scrapes Danny had had on his face the last time were healing up.

"You haven't had any more trouble?" D'Angelo asked.

"No, they've kept me segregated a lot of the time," Danny said. "You know what happens tomorrow, though. I get shipped off to Huntsville."

"Maybe, maybe not." D'Angelo leaned his head toward Phyllis. "Mrs. Newsom has something to ask you. Me, I don't know what it is, but I'm anxious to find out."

Danny's expression had been dull and dispirited when he came into the room, but now he looked more animated as he turned to Phyllis and asked, "What is it, Mrs. Newsom?"

"When Mike came to see you," Phyllis said, "you told him that you and Roxanne were planning to take a second honeymoon. Is that right?"

"Well, yeah," Danny said, frowning slightly. "We talked about it. Roxanne brought it up, and I told her we couldn't af-

248

ford it, but she said she'd been saving up and she thought we could. I was kind of surprised by that. I thought maybe she'd got a raise at the salon or something, although that Gibbs woman is so cheap you wouldn't think that was possible. I said if we had some extra money, we ought to use it to pay off some of our debt, but Roxanne said not to worry about that, she was going to take care of it."

Phyllis nodded and said, "But she never really explained where all that extra money was going to come from?"

"No, and I didn't press her on it. She seemed happy. We'd had a pretty rough time of it, so if she was feeling good about things, I didn't want to ruin that."

Phyllis leaned back and rested her hands on the metal table. "Thank you, Danny."

"That's it?" Danny looked both confused and disappointed.

Phyllis considered, then said, "One more thing. Did you know that Roxanne and Brian Flynn went to high school together?"

"What? No, Roxanne went to Brewer. Brian went to Western Hills."

"You know that for a fact?"

"Well, that's what she told me."

"You never saw her yearbook or anything like that?"

Danny's frown deepened. "No, she said her folks never bought any of them. They were too cheap for that, she told me." His hands, with plastic restraints around the wrists, clenched into fists. "Are you saying she lied?"

"I think maybe there were things about high school she didn't want to remember — like Brian. What happened first, did you and Brian go into business together, or were you and Roxanne married?"

"Brian and I opened the shop while Roxanne and I were dating."

"So you introduced her to him and they acted like they had never met before."

"Yeah, because they hadn't!" Danny shook his head. "This is nuts. You're saying Roxanne lied to me. What's next? Are you gonna say the two of them . . . that they —"

"Take it easy, Danny," D'Angelo said sharply. "If you get mad, the guards will come in and take you back to your cell, and I don't know if we're finished here."

"Danny, listen to me," Phyllis said. "There was nothing going on between Roxanne and Brian. I'm positive of that. She had her own reasons for not telling you the truth about where she went to school and knowing him, but there was nothing between them, you can be sure of that."

"I don't know anymore. I don't know about anything."

"You will. This is going to be over soon."

He looked and sounded like a little boy again as he said, "You promise?"

"I promise," Phyllis said, hoping she could keep it.

CHAPTER 22

Sam stood up from the bench where he was waiting in the jail lobby and asked, "Did you find out what you needed to know?"

"I did," Phyllis said as she and D'Angelo walked up, their footsteps echoing a little in the big room. "Roxanne acted like she did at the salon because she expected to get her hands on a considerable amount of money. Pauline Gibbs' instincts were right. I'm convinced Roxanne was going to quit. Remember how Mike said Danny told him they were going on a second honeymoon?"

"Yeah, come to think of it, I do."

"According to Danny, that windfall was going to pay for the trip *and* get them out of debt."

D'Angelo said, "You're just getting me more confused. Roxanne was a hair stylist. Where was she gonna get her hands on a bunch of money?"

"Brian Flynn can tell us that," Phyllis said.

"If he's at his shop today, and I think he will be."

Sam and D'Angelo looked at each other. Sam spread his hands and told the lawyer, "Might as well play along with her."

D'Angelo sighed. "Then I guess we're going to this paint and body shop. I don't know where it is —"

"I can tell you how to get there," Phyllis said.

A few minutes later, they were on the West Freeway, heading away from downtown. Phyllis used the time to mentally check back over every step of her theory. When she was finished, she knew it made sense and answered all the questions. She thought she knew how to prove it, too.

She navigated from the passenger seat and soon had D'Angelo approaching the paint and body shop. The doors on both repair bays were up, she saw. Brian had come to work today, just as she expected.

"Park in front of the office," she said, pointing. Then a thought occurred to her and she went on, "No, park in front of the bays, at an angle, so that you're blocking them."

"That's a little rude, isn't it?" D'Angelo said.

"There's a good reason for it."

He shrugged beefy shoulders and turned the wheel, angling the car off the road and bringing it to a stop where Phyllis had indicated.

Brian came out of the left-hand bay carrying one of the rubber mallets he used for beating dings out of fenders. He was moving slowly, and his face was pale and drawn as if he were sick or exhausted.

He managed to summon up a friendly smile, though, as Phyllis, Sam, and D'Angelo got out of the Caddy. He greeted them by saying, "I was about to tell you that you couldn't park there, but seeing as it's you, Mrs. Newsom . . ." Brian looked at D'Angelo. "Who's your friend?"

"This is Mr. D'Angelo, the attorney handling Danny's appeal," Phyllis said.

"Is that right?" Brian switched the mallet from his right hand to his left and extended the right. "It's a pleasure to meet you, sir. I hope you're doing a good job for Danny."

"Doing my best," D'Angelo said as he shook hands. "Right now, it seems like his fate is riding on Mrs. Newsom's shoulders."

Brian looked quizzically at Phyllis. "Is that right?"

"Yes, I've figured out a few things," Phyllis said. "For example, I know that you and Roxanne went to high school together."

"We did?" Brian seemed baffled. "I don't remember her from back then, and you'd think I would. Maybe we weren't in the same grade, though. And there were a lot of people at Western Hills. It's a big school."

"You graduated the same year. And you not only knew her, you dated her. The two of you were an item when you were the quarterback and she was captain of the cheerleaders. There's a yearbook picture to prove it."

Brian laughed and shook his head. "Okay, I definitely ought to remember that. But I swear, I don't. I guess maybe I smoked too much pot back in the old days." He looked at D'Angelo. "Will I get in trouble for admitting that in front of a lawyer?"

"I'm not interested in what you smoked," D'Angelo said. "I'm just trying to find out who killed Roxanne Jackson."

"Wait a minute." Brian was starting to look upset now. "You're not trying to say that *I* killed her, are you, Mrs. Newsom? Maybe Roxie and I dated back in high school, but there was nothing going on between us now —"

"We're not saying that there was," Phyllis told him. "And I don't think you killed Roxanne."

"Well, *that's* a relief —"

"D.J. Hutton killed her," Phyllis said. "Or to use her full name, Desiree Joan Hutton Chilton. But you're the one who shot her husband Hugh Chilton a couple of nights ago. At the very least, you'll be charged with conspiracy and attempted murder. If he dies, as is likely, the charge will be murder."

"Capital murder," D'Angelo added, picking up on what was going on well enough to back up Phyllis's play, even though he didn't know all the details yet.

Wide-eyed, Brian looked back and forth between them, then turned his shocked gaze toward Sam. "Mr. Fletcher, you seem like a level-headed guy. You haven't gone crazy enough to believe all this, have you?"

Sam shrugged and said, "It all adds up as far as I can see."

"Adds up? A friend of mine marries a girl I used to go out with in high school! Things like that probably happen all the time!"

"They probably do," Phyllis agreed. "Did you try to start something up with Roxanne again, after all these years?"

"Hell, no. Even if I'd wanted to, she wouldn't have had anything to do with it. I found out later she'd hated my guts for a long time." Brian grimaced as he realized that he'd just admitted recognizing Roxanne after all. In a defensive tone, he went on,

"Look, I had no idea she was pregnant back then. She never told me, and she sure as hell never told me about any miscarriage. All that was a long way behind us. We talked about it once and both agreed that for Danny's sake, we'd just leave the past buried, for good. I even tried not to spend any more time around her than I had to, just to make it easier for her."

"But you went with Danny to the salon a couple of times, and one of those times you recognized another old girlfriend: D.J. Hutton. You dated her before you went out with Roxanne. In fact, you dumped her in order to date Roxanne."

Brian shrugged. "I've always liked to play the field."

"No matter who got hurt."

"It was just high school romance, for God's sake! Nobody was supposed to take it seriously."

Phyllis said, "But it was different when you and D.J. met again after all this time. It *was* serious now. The two of you started having an affair. And Roxanne knew about it, probably because D.J. — Desiree — let something slip at the salon sometime. Roxanne knew that Desiree was a trophy wife, had married a man a lot older than her who had a lot of money. Maybe Roxanne and Desiree were friends now — a lot of old grudges tend to fade as the years pass — or maybe they just pretended to be and Desiree was still nursing a lot of anger toward her for taking you away from her. But even if they were friends, Roxanne wouldn't have let that stand in the way of what she saw as a way out of debt for her and Danny."

"She started blackmailing this other girl!" D'Angelo exclaimed as the light dawned for him.

Brian's face was more haggard than ever now, but he didn't say anything.

Phyllis continued, "Roxanne may have even found out about the plot you and Desiree hatched to murder her husband. She would leave the alarm off, you'd come in and shoot Hugh Chilton, ransack the place, and give her a minor wound to make it look like a botched home invasion. Was there some sort of stringent pre-nup so that Desiree couldn't get out of the marriage with any money? The police would have suspected her of being involved, of course, but they wouldn't know anything about you. They wouldn't be able to tie Desiree in with the person who actually pulled the trigger. It must have seemed like a risk worth running . . . until Desiree said too much to her old . . . what's the word?"

"Frenemy," Sam suggested.

"That's it. Her old frenemy from high school, who threatened to ruin everything unless she was paid off. Desiree must have decided she wasn't going to stand for that, so she went to the salon to have it out with Roxanne, and then all that old anger and resentment boiled to the surface, and . . ."

"Pow," D'Angelo said.

"Luckily, Danny came along to take the blame for the murder," Phyllis said. "You and Desiree held off on your murder plot until a couple of nights ago. She must have gotten spooked when you told her about how I was investigating Roxanne's death. She wanted her husband dead before anything else could turn up. But it didn't work out like the two of you planned. Hugh Chilton wounded you, badly enough that you didn't take the time to finish him off. You couldn't go to the emergency room or a doctor with a gunshot wound, so you patched it up yourself as best you could and came on to work today so everything would look normal here at the shop. I think the blood must have soaked through the bandage, though. I can see it on your coveralls."

Brian looked down sharply at his right side. There was nothing there.

"Aaaannd that'll just about do it," D'Angelo said. "No matter how much you and Mrs. Chilton tried to clean up, I'll bet you left some DNA on the scene, Flynn, and once we tip them off to check it against yours, that'll be all they need to arrest you. You think a woman like that's gonna go to bat for you, pal? She'll roll over on you so fast it'll make your head spin. She'll claim the whole thing was your idea and that she was so scared of you she had to go along with it. She'll probably even tell the cops it was *you* who killed Roxanne, not her."

Phyllis could tell by the horrified look in Brian's eyes that he knew D'Angelo was right. His lack of an apparent connection to the Chilton shooting had been the only thing keeping him safe. Once that link was exposed to the police, they would turn up the evidence they needed to convict him.

With an incoherent yell, Brian suddenly lunged at D'Angelo, swinging the rubber mallet.

Displaying surprising grace and agility for a man of his size and build, the lawyer ducked under the blow and hooked a hard left into Brian's side. Brian howled in pain and staggered back a step. Now there really was blood on his coveralls from the damage

D'Angelo's punch had done to the bullet wound.

Sam had slid over to get behind Brian. He grabbed him in a bear hug, pinning his arms to his sides. D'Angelo got hold of Brian, too, and together they forced him to the cement floor of the repair bay.

"We'll hang on to him!" D'Angelo said. "Call 911, Phyllis!"

"I already am," she said as she pushed the numbers on her cell phone.

Sam said, "This girl Desiree, D.J., whatever you call her, she was the one we saw kissin' Brian the other day?"

"That's right," Phyllis said. She and Sam were back in the living room of her house, where she had just laid out everything for Carolyn and Eve. "I should have recognized her then, and it took me a while to figure out why I didn't, since I was sitting just a few feet away from her at the beauty salon while I talked to her. But that day, I never saw her without some sort of herbal mask smeared all over her face. It covered up her features enough that when I saw her later, without it and with her hair different, I didn't know her right away. And I certainly didn't recognize her as the cheerleader D.J. Hutton from that yearbook photo. Now that

I know, I can see the resemblance, but . . ."

"What's going to happen now?" Eve asked. "Are they going to let Danny go?"

"Mr. D'Angelo has filed a motion to have Danny's conviction set aside and the charges against him dropped, and as soon as a judge grants that, he'll be a free man again." Phyllis paused. "A free man with a murdered wife, a business partner who's in jail, and the knowledge that the woman he loved turned out to be a blackmailer." She shook her head. "It's better than being locked up for a crime he didn't commit, but it's not really what you'd call a happy ending for him, either."

"Happy endings are overrated," Carolyn said. "It's justice that's important."

"Never hurts to have a little bit of both," Sam said.

"Why didn't they just wait to try to murder the woman's husband?" Carolyn went on. "If they hadn't done that, you never would have seen that newspaper story and might not have solved the crime."

Eve said, "Phyllis would have solved it some other way. I'm sure of that."

"I'm not," Phyllis said with a slight smile. "I had figured out that Roxanne must have been blackmailing someone, and whoever it was, most likely was the killer. Maybe I would have narrowed it down to Desiree Chilton eventually, but who knows? Once Brian told her the case might not be as closed as they thought it was, Desiree panicked. Just like she lost her head and her temper that evening the salon after Roxanne let her in. She lashed out. This time it's probably going to cost Mrs. Chilton her freedom for the rest of her life."

"They're testifying against each other?" Eve asked.

"Singin' like birdies," Sam said with a grin. "To hear both of them tell it, the other one's the mastermind. I reckon the cops and the courts will get it all sorted out eventually." He put his hands on his knees and got ready to push himself up from the sofa. "In the meantime, I got a kindergartner to go pick up. You think when we get back, we could maybe have a slice o' that pie?"

Phyllis smiled and said, "I think that could be arranged."

■ ■ ■ ■ ■

RECIPES

■ ■ ■ ■

BANANA BLUEBERRY OATMEAL MUG

Ingredients

1 teaspoon coconut oil
1 egg
2 tablespoons cream cheese
2/3 cup instant oatmeal
3 tablespoons milk
2 tablespoons maple syrup
1/2 banana, mashed
1/4 cup blueberries

Directions

Mix well in a large 20 oz. mug. Microwave for 2 1/2-3 minutes.

BACON TOMATO PIE

Ingredients

Pie Crust

1 1/4 cups all-purpose flour

1/4 cup cold vegetable shortening, cut into pieces

4 tablespoons cold unsalted butter, cut into pieces

1/2 teaspoon garlic salt

3 to 4 Tbsp. ice-cold water

Filling

2 pounds tomatoes, thinly sliced

1 1/4 teaspoons salt, divided

4-6 slices bacon (reserve 1 tablespoon bacon grease)

1 onion, chopped

1/2 teaspoon freshly ground pepper, divided

1/2 cup assorted chopped fresh herbs (such as chives, parsley, and basil)

1 cup fresh spinach leaves

1/2 cup freshly grated Gruyère cheese

1/2 cup freshly grated Parmigiano-Reggiano cheese

1/4 cup cream cheese

Directions

Pie crust: With a pastry blender, cut shortening and butter into the flour until mixture resembles coarse meal.

Gradually add 3 tablespoons ice-cold water, 1 tablespoon at a time, and process until dough forms a ball and leaves sides of bowl, add 1 more tablespoon water, if necessary. Shape dough into a disk, and wrap in plastic wrap, and chill 30 minutes.

Unwrap dough, and place on a lightly floured surface; sprinkle lightly with flour. Roll dough to 1/8-inch thickness.

Preheat oven to 425°F. Press dough into a 9-inch pie plate. Trim dough 1 inch larger than diameter of pie plate; fold overhanging dough under itself along rim of pie plate. Chill 30 minutes or until firm.

Line the dough with parchment paper or foil. Fill the parchment or foil with pie weights, uncooked rice or dried beans. Place on baking sheet.

Bake at 425°F for 20 minutes. Remove weights and parchment paper or foil. Bake 5 minutes or until browned. Cool completely on baking sheet on a wire rack (about 30 minutes). Reduce oven temperature to 350°F.

Filling: Place tomatoes in a single layer on paper towels; sprinkle with 1 tsp. salt. Let stand 15 minutes.

Sauté onion and 1/4 tsp. each salt and pepper in hot bacon grease in a skillet over medium heat until onion is tender.

Start with a layer of spinach leaves on the bottom of the pie crust. Remove any big stems. Pat tomatoes dry with a paper towel. Layer tomatoes, onion, and herbs in prepared crust, lightly seasoning each layer with pepper. Crumble the bacon and sprinkle on the last layer. Stir together grated cheeses and cream cheese; spread over pie.

Bake at 350°F for 30 minutes or until lightly browned, shielding edges with foil to prevent excessive browning. Serve hot, warm, or at room temperature.

Makes 6 to 8 servings

SPINACH SALAD

Ingredients
1 10 oz. bag baby spinach (washed)
1/3 cup sweetened dried cranberries
1/4 cup chopped walnuts
2 pears peeled and chopped
1/2 cup blue cheese crumbles
4 tablespoons coconut oil
2 teaspoons fresh lime juice
1 teaspoon sugar

Directions
Wash and dry the spinach. Add spinach and next 4 ingredients, and toss gently.

In a small bowl combine coconut oil, lime juice and sugar, stirring well. Add oil mixture to salad; toss to coat.

Serves 4-6

CHICKEN STUFFED JALAPEÑO POPPERS

Ingredients
4 slices cooked bacon crumbled
6 skinless chicken breast
8 ounces cream cheese, softened
1 cup shredded cheddar cheese
2-3 jalapenos, seeded and finely chopped
1 green onion, finely chopped

Directions
Preheat oven to 425°F degrees.

Split each chicken breast down the middle, but not all the way through.

In a bowl, mix the bacon, cream cheese, cheddar cheese, peppers and green onion.

Spoon about 1/6th of the mixture into each breast.

Bake 20-25 minutes in the preheated oven,

until bubbly and lightly browned.

Serves 6

AVOCADO SALAD

Ingredients
2 cups cherry tomatoes, split in half
2 cucumbers, sliced
1/2 red onion, sliced
2 avocados — peeled, pitted and diced
8 ounces mozzarella cheese half inch cubes
1/4 cup basil, chopped *
2 tablespoons olive oil
2 tablespoons lemon juice

Directions
Put tomatoes, cucumbers, red onion, avocado, mozzarella, and basil into a large salad bowl.

Drizzle with olive oil and lemon juice. Toss gently to combine. Just before serving, toss

* You can use cilantro instead of basil.

with 1/2 tsp sea salt and 1/8 tsp black pepper.

Serves 4-6

CHOCOLATE CHERRY SLAB PIE

Ingredients

Filling
3 pounds cherries
1 cup sugar
3 tablespoons cornstarch
1.5 cups chocolate chips

Crust
8 cups flour
1 cup sugar
2 teaspoons salt
1 pound cold unsalted butter (4 sticks)
3 eggs
1/2 cup cold water
Heavy cream or egg wash, for brushing the crust
Confectioners' sugar, for dusting (optional)

Directions

Preheat the oven to 400°F. Butter one 13 × 18-inch sheet pan. Set aside another to use as a template.

Filling: Put the cherries in a large bowl. In a small bowl, whisk together the sugar and cornstarch until well combined. Add the sugar mixture to the cherries and gently toss. Set aside.

Crust: In a large bowl, whisk together the flour, sugar, and salt. Cut sticks of chilled butter into pieces. With a pastry blender, cut in butter, working until mixture resembles coarse meal.

In a separate bowl, whisk the eggs with the cold water. Make a well in the middle of the flour mixture, then pour the egg mixture into the well. Working from the center out, combine the egg and flour mixtures until the dough holds together. If necessary, adjust by adding a little additional flour or cold water if the dough is too sticky or not holding together.

Divide the dough into two balls, one almost twice the size of the other.

On a large floured surface, roll out the

larger portion of dough to an 18 × 22-inch rectangle (roll it out slightly larger, then trim the edges straight to the correct dimensions). Dust the dough with flour a few times while rolling out to keep the dough from sticking.

Wrap the dough around the rolling pin, then unroll it over the first sheet pan. Adjust the dough so it sits evenly in the sheet pan. Dock the pastry by pricking it with a fork across the bottom and sides of the pastry. Spread the chocolate chips in an even layer over the pastry. Spread the cherry mixture in an even layer on top of the chips. Set aside.

Roll out the smaller dough portion to a rectangle just larger than 13 × 18 inches. Flip the second sheet pan upside down and gently press it into the dough, then lift the pan off. Use the impression to cut the dough to size. Gently wrap it around the rolling pin, then unroll it over the slab pie to form a top crust.

Fold excess dough from the crust bottom up and around to meet the pie top and gently pinch the crust to form the top edge. Brush the top and the edges of the pastry with cream (or egg wash). Cut slits into the top of the slab pie for vents.

Bake for 30 to 40 minutes, or until the top is golden. Remove the pie from the oven and allow to cool. Dust with confectioners' sugar (if desired), slice, and serve.

KID FRIENDLY GUACAMOLE

Ingredients

4 ripe avocados
1 lemon (freshly squeezed lemon juice)
2 dashes hot pepper sauce
1 small red onion, diced
1 large garlic clove, minced
1 teaspoon salt
1 teaspoon freshly ground black pepper
1 medium tomato, seeded, and diced

Directions

Cut the avocados in half, remove the pits. Use the knife to cut up the avocados in their peels cutting down to the peel but not through it. Scoop the flesh out of their peels into a large bowl. The avocado should be in chunks now. Add the lemon juice, hot pepper sauce, onion, garlic, salt, and pepper and toss well. Using a sharp knife, slice through the avocados in the bowl until they are finely diced. Add the tomatoes. Mix well and taste for salt and pepper.

(If you want it to have more of a kick, add more hot sauce)

Makes 3 cups.

BLACK AND BLUEBERRY PIE

Ingredients

Pie Crust
2 1/2 cups all-purpose flour
1/2 teaspoon salt
1 cup butter, chilled and diced
1/2 cup ice water

Directions

In a large mixing bowl, combine flour and salt. Cut in butter until mixture resembles coarse crumbs. Stir in water, a tablespoon at a time, until mixture forms a ball. (Use only as much water as needed.) Divide dough into two balls and wrap in plastic wrap. Refrigerate overnight.

Roll both balls of dough out to fit a 9 inch pie plate. Place bottom crust in pie plate. Press the dough evenly into the bottom and sides of the pie plate.

Ingredients

Filling
2 cups fresh blackberries
3 cups fresh blueberries
1/2 cup white sugar
1/2 cup all-purpose flour
1 beaten egg
1 tablespoon lemon juice
1 tablespoon butter chopped
1/4 cup white sugar

Directions
Preheat oven to 425 degrees F.

Brush the bottom crust with some of the beaten egg. Combine 4 1/2 cups berries with the sugar and flour well until you no longer see any white coating on the berries. Spoon the mixture into the bottom crust. Spread the remaining 1/2 cup berries on top of the sweetened berries. Squeeze lemon juice over the filling and dot berries with small chunks of butter. Cover with the top crust, seal and crimp the edges, and cut vents in the top crust for steam to escape.

Brush the top crust with more of the beaten egg, and sprinkle with 1/4 cup sugar.

Bake in the preheated oven for 15 minutes.

Reduce the temperature of the oven to 375 degrees F (190 degrees C), and bake for an additional 20 to 25 minutes, or until the filling is bubbly and the crust is golden brown. Cool on wire rack.

SLOW COOK
HONEY SESAME CHICKEN

Ingredients

2-3 pounds boneless, skinless chicken
  breasts, cut in 1 inch chunks
Salt and pepper
2 cups pineapple chunks (canned, frozen,
  or fresh)
1 cup honey
1/4 cup light soy sauce
3 tablespoons diced red onion
4 tablespoons ketchup
2 tablespoon coconut oil
3 cloves garlic, minced
Red pepper flakes (optional)
4 teaspoons cornstarch dissolved in 4 tablespoons water
Sesame seeds

Directions

Use a liner or lightly oil slow cooker.

Season chicken with lightly with salt and

pepper, and place in the bottom of slow cooker. Add pineapple to the slow cooker.

Mix in a small bowl, honey, soy sauce, onion, ketchup, oil, garlic and pepper flakes and stir until well combined. Pour over chicken.

Cook on low for 3 hours, or just until chicken is cooked through.

Dissolve 4 teaspoons of cornstarch in 4 tablespoons of water and pour into crock pot. Stir to combine with sauce. Replace lid and cook sauce on high for fifteen minutes or until thickened.

Sprinkle with sesame seeds and serve over rice.

Serves 6.

ABOUT THE AUTHOR

Livia J. Washburn has been a professional writer for more than twenty years. She received the Private Eye Writers of America Award and the American Mystery Award for her first mystery, *Wild Night*, written under the name L. J. Washburn, and she was nominated for a Spur Award by the Western Writers of America for a novel written with her husband, James Reasoner. Her short story "Panhandle Freight" was nominated for a Peacemaker Award by the Western Fictioneers, and her story "Charlie's Pie" won. She lives with her husband in a small Texas town, where she is constantly experimenting with new recipes. Her two grown daughters are both teachers in her hometown, and she is very proud of them.

The employees of Thorndike Press hope you have enjoyed this Large Print book. All our Thorndike, Wheeler, and Kennebec Large Print titles are designed for easy reading, and all our books are made to last. Other Thorndike Press Large Print books are available at your library, through selected bookstores, or directly from us.

For information about titles, please call:
  (800) 223-1244

or visit our website at:
  gale.com/thorndike

To share your comments, please write:
Publisher
Thorndike Press
10 Water St., Suite 310
Waterville, ME 04901